I0550101

The

Reluctant Prince

A Prince Tale

Author: Edithe Kingsburrow

Preface

As King Stefen entered the morning room, he felt a change in the atmosphere. Something had happened, but what? As he surveyed the room for his wife, Queen Hannah, he saw a beautiful bouquet of flowers sitting on the small table where she usually breakfasted. Instantly he knew it had come from her home and neighboring Kingdom, Breckridge Hall.

Immediately he searched the table for a parchment. While he loved that his wife and her friend, Queen Lydia, enjoyed communicating through flowers, he preferred words. He felt that words avoided miscommunication. No need to borrow trouble. Finding the unfolded parchment, he read quickly.

My Dearest Hannah,

Markus and I have been blessed with a beautiful daughter, only a fortnight ago. Markus was going to send word right after her birth, but I wanted to tell you myself.

I hope that you and Stefen will share in our joy.

With love,

Lydia.

Stefen folded the parchment, returned it to the table and with a sigh, he said, "I must see Hannah."

Hannah had desperately wanted more children. Of course, he knew she would be happy for Lydia and Markus, but this would only remind her of their loss. This would be difficult, and he did not want her to face it alone. He knew where she would be.

Hannah was on a bench in her favorite place, her gardens. The solitude of her private gardens always seemed to bring her peace and inspiration. He quietly sat next to her and put his arm around her waist. It was not long before she gave a sigh and laid her head on his strong, broad shoulders. For a time neither of them spoke. The silence engulfed them.

Sitting in the quiet of the gardens you could hear the bees as they flew busily from flower to flower. *This must be a paradise for these bees,* thought Stefen. *This garden would not be so lovely without them.* The monarch found himself smiling as he thought of the many bouquets that Hannah had gathered herself and sent to friends, family and even strangers. Why even now, he was sure that she was mentally organizing a bouquet for this very occasion.

Finally Queen Hannah broke the silence, "I am very happy for them. You know that don't you?"

"Of course dear, and so am I."

"Do you now regret the arrangement we made seven years ago? Lydia could have given you another child."

"You know I do not! There are no guarantees. Accidents happen- our life together is as it should be. Hannah, what must I do to convince you that you and you alone are my only love? I know that our courtship was not what either of us had ever dreamt of. However, speaking at least for myself, I am so much happier than a man, prince or pauper, has a right to be. Are you unhappy, Hannah?"

"Oh Stefen, I love you with all of my heart." And taking a deep breath, she brushed a tear away and whispered, "I desperately wanted to have at least one more child."

Stefen gave her a tight squeeze, "I know, dearest." Then with a mischievous smile he said, "Prince Carlton is so active. He is only five years and he keeps Matilda and his nanny running practically all day! Why, I think they have both lost at least one stone and if we don't take care he will wear them out!" The King chuckled as the gate to the gardens burst open and Carlton ran in with his nanny trailing close behind him.

Seeking freedom from the nanny, Carlton ran into his mother's arms tattling. "Mummy, Nanny Sarah won't let me ride Thunder!"

Queen Hannah, scooped him into her arms and kissed his forehead gently. After a quick hug she put him down and took his small dimpled hands in hers. "Carlton, guess what, King Markus and Queen Lydia have just had a new baby girl!

"Does that mean that Prince Everett has a little sister?" asked the little Prince.

"Yes Carlton, do you want to help mummy gather a bouquet to send to them."

Just as King Stefen suspected, Hannah picked up her shears and began snipping Iris' in a variety of colors.

"What will this bouquet say?" asked King Stefen.

As Hannah added a branch of parsley and sage, she held the flowers in Stefen's direction. "Just as we feel! We are so pleased with your good news! I just need to add some rosemary and thyme."

A smile broke out on her face as she continued, "I'm putting in some pansies too. Her little Princess is bound to be whimsical!"

Stefen chuckled as he continued to watch Hannah composing the bouquet. This practice of communicating with flowers was not old, but rarely used as much as Hannah and Lydia used it. They were always sending messages back and forth with flowers. He knew that Hannah would not be sad long. She very seldom thought of herself. This was only one of her many gifts that made him fall in love with her. Oh, how he loved her.

Seeing that she had cheered herself, he quietly slipped out of the gardens, beckoning for Carlton and his nanny to join him. They would to leave her to work her magic without distraction.

The Reluctant Prince

Part 1

Twenty Years Later

"Why did he have to go and do that?" Prince Carlton asked his valet. "It ruined everything!"

"What did the King do now, Your Highness?"

"Oh, just as the meal came to an end, he announced that Princess Caroline will be coming to visit in two months' time!"

"Princess Caroline? The one to whom you are betrothed?"

"Exactly! Why did he have to go and ruin everything?"

"Your Highness doesn't want to see her?"

"Of course not! Why should I? I am still young! I know that my father is determined to turn this betrothal into a ridiculous engagement. Now all of the courtiers are sure to avoid me."

"Have you ever met Princess Caroline Your Highness? When was the betrothal made?"

"Yes, I have met her, at least ten years ago. Our parents arranged our marriage at her birth.

"I am friends with her brother, Prince Everett. You know him, we used to play together when I was younger, we studied together at University and from time to time we still go on a hunt. However, I haven't visited Breckridge Hall for several years!

"All I remember about the princess, is that she is five years my junior. I am not ready to settle down yet! I am only 25 years old. I enjoy the attention I get from all of the courtiers at every assembly and ball. Why should I be forced to end all that now?"

"Maybe Princess Caroline will be worth settling down for."

"Really, Thorndyke, you were my whipping boy too long! She can't be much to look at, or why the early betrothal?"

"That's a great question, Your Highness." Not wanting to show disrespect for the Prince and his ignorance with regard to protocol, Thorndyke responded, "Why were you betrothed to her and how does she feel about it? Maybe she feels the same way you do. Perhaps both of your parents were too hasty, and could be convinced to reconsider."

"You may just have something there, Thorndyke! Ring for Matilda!"

"Yes Your Highness."

Matilda had been the housekeeper in the castle for as long as Prince Carlton could remember. She surely would know the details of the Prince's betrothal. Matilda was middle-aged and very energetic. She always seemed genuinely pleased to help the Prince with anything he asked of her.

"Matilda, what do you know about the Princess Caroline?" asked Prince Carlton.

"We'll, Your Highness, the last time we saw her she was only ten. She seemed to be comely, for a young girl, but I have not heard anything about her since their last visit. After your grandfather passed away, it was difficult for your parents to visit Breckridge Hall. The demands of ruling the Kingdoms and the distance between Cantwell and Breckridge Hall made it difficult."

"Thank you, Matilda."

Matilda bowed and then looked at the Prince as if she wanted to say more.

"What is it Matilda? You may speak freely."

"The King is sending a messenger to Breckridge Hall, inviting the Royal family here for the Fall Festival. I can arrange for the messenger to bring you word upon his return. He could ask the servants for details about Princess Caroline, if you like."

Carlton was formulating a plan in his mind. "That is an excellent idea, Matilda. Who is he sending?"

"Hilbert, Your Highness. He will leave at first light. Shall I speak with him?"

"Thank you, no I will speak with him myself before I retire. Thank you, Matilda."

Prince Carlton waited until Matilda left the room and the door had closed completely.

Disappointed with the lack of information, but with a plan in mind, Carlton exploded. "Thorndyke, pack our bags! You and I are accompanying Hilbert to Breckridge Hall."

"You are going to see Princess Caroline? Without being properly invited? The King will never allow it!"

"Calm down, Thorndyke. I am going incognito. I will say we are going hunting. We will ride with Hilbert as far as the Ram's Head Inn. With a small deception, I will visit the servants and see just what kind of a hand I have been dealt! After I have learned about the Princess, we will hunt whatever you choose."

Thorndyke began packing while Prince Carlton sent word to Hilbert to expect them to accompany him as far as The Ram's Head Inn.

Part 2

Prince Carlton and his two companions reached the inn about an hour after sundown. Hilbert decided to spend the night at the inn and complete his journey the following morning. The Prince determined that he would wait for Hilbert to deliver the parchment and begin his trek back to Cantwell before he approached Breckridge Hall.

Finally sure that Hilbert was on his way back to the Castle, Prince Carlton made his way to the servant's entrance of the kitchens. It was early afternoon. This would be a great time to speak with the servants. He insisted that Thorndyke wait for him at the inn, Prince Carlton felt it would look better if he went alone, dressed as a man's servant. He took a deep breath and rang the bell. After a few minutes a young servant girl answered the door.

"May I sit for a spell?" he asked. "I have been travelling all morning. My feet could certainly use a rest and my eyes never tire when they are feasting on such a pretty face."

The girl appeared slightly over dressed for a servant, but she was pleasant to look at. Her long brown hair was pulled back just enough to see her beautiful brown eyes. She was slender and had a slight turned up nose. Her complexion was flawless, which was surprising for a scullery maiden. Though she was pretty, Prince Carlton never lacked for speech; and he always had plenty of compliments to bestow on a pretty girl.

The maiden kindly offered him a chair, however she did not take kindly to his flattering words nor did she seem impressed with his compliments. She actually appeared to be more annoyed with him than anything.

At first this concerned the Prince. Was he losing his touch? He quickly dismissed that notion, deciding that it was not his lack of charm, but more likely that this poor servant was not used to receiving a man's attention and did not know how to respond to his compliments.

He would get on with the mission at hand. After all, he never lacked for a pretty girl's attention, he did not need to waste time on her, especially a lowly servant.

"What can you tell me about your mistress, Princess Caroline?"

With an underlying smile, the maiden quickly turned the conversation around.

"Why speak of the Princess? I have heard tell she is betrothed. Who are you to pursue such information?"

Completely ignoring the last question, the Prince queried, "Oh, to whom?"

"Oh, a feeble, old Prince, so it is rumored. She does not recall him."

This caught Prince Carlton off guard. While it might have occurred to him that the Princess may not want to marry him, he never thought of himself as old or feeble!

"Why are they betrothed, if he is so old? I heard tell the Prince is only five years her senior. Is that not so?"

"So, you knew she was betrothed? If you are so knowledgeable, why did you bother to ask me?"

Had the Prince foiled his mission already? He was not used to this type of conversation, especially from a servant. Generally he was allowed any mode of decorum of speech. No one ever challenged his right to receive information, or anything for that matter. He had never been denied anything since his early youth.

Taking a breath, he remembered that this servant did not know who or what he was. If he was to gain the information he desired, he would have to allow verbal sparring with this maiden.

"I confess, I have heard of the betrothal, to Prince Carlton of Cantwell is that not so? I have heard that he is only 25 years of age."

"That is what they say, but he must be a sickly fellow, or maimed in some way" said the servant girl, in a matter of fact tone.

"Why do you say that?" asked the Prince.

But he was denied an answer, for at that moment, the back door bell on the service entrance rang twice. Instead of her response to his question, she said. "I am sorry sir, but it is time for the servants to prepare for the evening meal. I am afraid you will have to leave."

Before he knew it, and not quite sure how it happened, Prince Carlton was standing just outside the servant's door as it shut - the young maiden, nowhere to be seen. Within minutes there were at least half a dozen maidens and two huntsmen coming to the door.

"May we help you sir?" asked an elderly woman.

The Prince fumbled for words, then composing himself replied, "I came to inquire...no thank you, I will return tomorrow."

Prince Carlton excused himself and went back to the inn. He had hoped that he would have been able to have a few questions answered and be on his way. He could have spoken with another servant, but Thorndyke had warned him to only speak to one servant, in private. He mentioned that most all of the servants in a household such as a castle are fiercely loyal to their royal families and if he truly wanted to gather information about the Princess, he would have to be selective in which servant he addressed.

Not considering his valet's counsel, he spoke with the first pretty girl he saw. The Prince thought he had a way with girls and was sure that she would be spilling all of the *royal secrets* after just a few flattering comments. If the bell had not rung for the servants to begin preparing for the evening meal, Prince Carlton felt sure he would have had all the goods on Princess Caroline. Now he would have to wait until tomorrow, one more visit to their kitchens and then they could go hunting!

The next afternoon, Prince Carlton arrived a full half an hour earlier than he had the previous day. He decided to take a different approach with the scullery maid. *After all,* he told himself, *maiden or queen all women are alike!* After giving a solid knock at the servant's door, he smiled to himself, quite pleased with his new plan and confident of a satisfactory outcome.

Just as he had hoped, the same maiden came to the door. She was not as pleasant as she had been the day before, but she did allow the Prince to enter and sit at the table as she finished her baking.

This was not at all how he had imagined, he thought she would be more pleased to see him. But with all of the charm he could muster and still consider himself a servant, he again asked about her mistress, Princess Caroline.

The maiden, seeing that he was determined, became equally charming as she described the princess. "She is a very particular and loving woman, especially where her suitors are concerned. She is determined to have a union or marriage very similar to that of her parents and insists that her betrothal to Prince Carlton is in every way a mock of marriage and Kingdom."

This was a great comfort to the Prince and just as he prepared to leave, the maiden began to expound on the reasons why Prince Carlton was not a worthy companion for her mistress. She went on until the bell rang and he was, as he had been the day before, quickly ushered out of the kitchen. Had the Prince left just a few minutes earlier, he would have been a completely happy man.

Part 3

Thorndyke saw the Prince approaching and had a man there to take his horse to the stables. The valet then followed Prince Carlton to his room and quickly poured water in the basin and helped him change his clothes.

"Did it go well, Your Highness?" asked Thorndyke, as he finished tying the Princes' cravat.

"No! Not at all." said the Prince, obviously frustrated. "The scullery maiden as much as said that Princess Caroline will do everything in her power to cancel the betrothal!"

Confused, Thorndyke asked, "Isn't that good? I thought that was what you wanted."

"It was, well at least at first. How can she say I am an unworthy suitor? She doesn't even know me!"

Before his valet could respond, the Prince continued. "Do you think I am a fop? That I am lazy? That I will be a poor excuse for a monarch? Does the entire Kingdom question my ability to lead? Thorndyke, I am in no mood to go hunting! We must return to the castle at once!"

"I will pack and have the horses readied, Your Highness."

Carlton needed private time for some serious reflection. He spent most of Sunday in his private chamber, leaving only to attended church, this he did to see if he could get direction and insight.

He was insulted at the presumptuous conclusions made against him. Carlton determined to "see what was going on in his Kingdom." *Unworthy*! *I could do anything I put my mind to – I don't really care that she doesn't want to marry me, I don't want to marry her. Did those comments about his character represent attitudes and opinions of the masses, or only her Highness, Princess Caroline?*

The next morning, King Stefen was surprised, but pleased, when Prince Carlton joined him in the throne room. Monday mornings were set aside for the King to hear the concerns and complaints of his people. Carlton had been invited and encouraged to attend ever since his 16th birthday. However, the Prince seemed to have other priorities and rarely attended. He had always been too busy or too tired to make this tradition a part of his weekly schedule.

It was for good reason the Prince had not participated in his father's affairs. It was his opinion that his father had surrendered his freedom to tedious and dull activities; yet now, Carlton determined he would make an effort to understand the workings of ruling a Kingdom. After all, his father was a happy man; he appeared to enjoy his work.

As Prince Carlton sat next to his father, he listened intently to the concerns of the people. Admittedly, at first, Carlton found himself scrutinizing their apparel. He had to force himself to look past their choice of fashion and focus on their concerns. He did take note that none of the people wore rags. He felt this was a reflection of the goodness of his father. He was quite proud of the fact that his father was a good King and leader. He did not glut himself on the labors of his people. Taxes were modest and the people loved him. None of the people in their Kingdom were poor. Some had more than others, but it was more a reflection of their choices. As he listened, it was difficult, at first. It was hard for the Prince not to interrupt, to curb his desire to say, "What do you expect? You did it to yourself!"

Listening to their concerns, he saw the love his father had for these people. He genuinely sought to protect their welfare and happiness. The disputes were minor and always settled to the satisfaction of everyone. Carlton had never witnessed this side of his father nor had he realized the wisdom and the respect that a King must have for his subjects, if they are to live in peace and unity.

Realizing that wisdom is a trait he would like to acquire, Carlton decided he would take the opportunity to learn all he could from his father. When it was his time to reign as King, he would like to have wisdom and a love for the people of his Kingdom. He would like them to love him, as he had witnessed their love for his father.

The more he reflected on the accusations of the scullery maid, he was forced to admit that perhaps they were partially true. As he sat with his father listening to the stories and struggles of his people, he saw similarities in himself. He had misjudged these people who had come to the throne room seeking resolution to their problems.

One man, in particular felt he was more entitled to a grazing field than his neighbor. To him, his neighbor's animals were of a lesser breed, or inferior to his own. Carlton's first thought was, "How pompous!" But immediately he remembered the hunting bow he demanded although it had been made for someone else simply because he was the Prince. On occasion, Carlton had used his station unfairly. Hearing their complaints was sometimes like looking into a mirror, he didn't like what he saw.

For the next few weeks Prince Carlton made sure he was in the throne room every Monday. He began to see everything in a different light. After a few weeks, he could see the effects of his father's council and enjoyed listening to the people as they returned to the King bearing gifts and expressing gratitude. The gifts that once seemed so ridiculous were now recognized for what they were, expressions of love and thankfulness. These people were happy. They loved their good King and sharing their crafts or harvest with him was a sincere demonstration of their affection.

The Prince continued to exercise his horse daily and now as he did so, he began taking an interest in the cottages as he passed. He began to recognize some of the people who had come to the throne room. On one such a day, a farmer beckoned him to come and see his new foal. With great pride this man escorted Prince Carlton to his pasture where a mare stood lovingly watching her new filly as she pranced in the paddock. Then with tears in his eyes he showed Carlton a beautiful stack of hay. He explained that he was able to harvest so much because the King had implemented a crop share amongst the farmers.

This decree encouraged the farmers to work together during the planting and harvesting seasons; enabling them to work more ground and enjoy a greater harvest. Even those who did not own property were able to hire out and would receive produce or hay as their pay. This had been going on for several years. The crop share was partially responsible for the peace that their Kingdom now enjoyed.

Prince Carlton, was no longer amazed at the love the people had for their King, his father. They were responding to the love and respect that he had always shown to them.

The sixth week, a middle aged man came to the throne room. He said he had a problem with his stallion. After receiving permission to address the King, he respectfully asked for Prince Carlton's advice. At first this took the Prince by surprise, but as he reflected on it, he realized that his father rarely went to the stables any more. He occasionally found time to hunt with Carlton, but then, had never enjoyed the mews like Carlton did. The Prince spent hours working with the horses. His father had given him charge over the stables several years ago. Prince Carlton was well known for his knowledge and love of horses. His personal horse was admired wherever he went.

After learning of the man's concern, Carlton was able to give him advice about his horse. He also requested that the man return in two weeks' time, with a report. This earned a smile of satisfaction from the King.

Time passed quickly. Soon the castle was bustling with excitement as preparations were being made for the arrival of Princess Caroline and her family: King Markus, Queen Lydia and Prince Everett of Breckridge Hall.

Prince Carlton was anxious, too. Would the Princess really reject him as her servant had suggested? Thorndyke had tried to console him; however, he still felt anxious for her arrival. He was still lamenting all the insults he had received from the servant. He would just have to wait for her arrival and judge for himself. The Prince had been so busy, trying to disprove the accusations against him that he had forgotten to find out more about Princess Caroline.

Carlton would not meet the royal family upon their arrival. On an occasion such as this, the betrothed couple would not see each other until the Assembly Ball. This suited Carlton as he was hoping that the Princess would see him for the man that he really was. He would be dressed to the hilt and though he may appear somewhat arrogant, he knew that no maiden would find his appearance displeasing. Carlton did not want to appear anxious to meet her, nor did he want to spare her the embarrassment she would surely feel when she met him at the ball, then she could see for herself that he was not as 'old' or 'feeble' as she had thought.

Carlton had heard the Minstrel's song since his early manhood, and if the Minstrel was correct, "No maiden could help but swoon in his presence!"

The Prince smiled vainly as he recalled the last four lines of the sonnet:

"But what woman, young or old would wince

For none can help but beam,

When she first lays eyes on our most handsome Prince

For all are left to Dream"

Part 4

The ball began with a grandeur that had never been witnessed by anyone in attendance. No doubt this was because of the King's intentions to announce the engagement of his son, heir to the throne. Protocol would not allow anything less. All of the local gentry had accepted their invitations and had arrived promptly. The ballroom was nearly full when King Stefen and Queen Hannah arrived. Prince Carlton, would normally arrive just prior to his parents, but with an announcement of this occasion, he would be presented after his parents and just prior to the Princess Caroline.

The Prince dressed in his best suit and cravat. His family banner was proudly displayed in a royal blue sash across his chest.

As he descended the stairs, all eyes were admiring him in his uniform and stately manner. The courtiers swooned and Prince Carlton was annoyed with it all. For the first time in his life, he looked at these ladies with displeasure. He was not flattered by their attention or meaningless conversations.

Filled with frustration, Carlton thought, *how could this poppet of a princess have such an influence on my emotions? We have never even engaged in conversation.* Prince Carlton found himself waiting anxiously for the arrival of Princess Caroline.

When he heard the voice of the Lord High Steward, "His majesty, King Markus and Her Highness, Queen Lydia of Breckridge Hall", Carlton took a deep breath.

Everyone bowed and curtsied as the royal couple descended the stairs and finally came to a halt in front of Carlton and his parents, King Stefen and Queen Hannah of Cantwell.

"His Highness, Prince Everett of Cantwell." The Lord High Steward announced with enthusiasm.

Seeing Prince Everett helped put Carlton somewhat at ease. The two men clasped forearms and exchanged pleasantries before they heard the last drum of the Steward.

Only moments later all eyes turned to the top of the staircase as the steward, using his staff, drummed the floor announcing the long awaited arrival of the, "Princess Caroline of Breckridge Hall."

There was an audible gasp, as the beautiful, young princess descended the stairs. Surprisingly, Carlton immediately recognized the Princess, and he chuckled smugly to himself. She was, in fact the scullery maid he had talked with in the kitchens of Breckridge Hall!

Carlton was not disappointed by this turn of events. He may have some undesirable qualities, but he now knew for a fact that Princess Caroline took liberties not of her station. A princess would never trespass into the kitchens to perform labors that were reserved for those born to that station. Carlton was curious to learn if the King and Queen, her parents, were aware of this error in decorum or if the Princess had been able to keep this habit hidden from them. Regardless, Prince Carlton was certain that this formal meeting was off to a good start. Once again, he had the upper hand.

Princess Caroline was the scullery maid. This information, had quite the opposite effect on him. He was pleased by her appearance and fascinated by her forthright personality. He looked forward to spending the next few weeks, playfully sparring vocally with the bold, beautiful princess.

After the official introductions were made, King Stefen motioned for the musicians to begin. As was expected, Prince Carlton offered his arm to Princess Caroline and led her to the center of the dance floor. The ball began with the traditional waltz, King Stefen and King Markus led their wives to the floor shortly after the third set.

Distracted by the beauty of the hall and the anticipation of her future, her destiny, Caroline did not recognize the Prince, at first. She had a nagging feeling that she had talked with him before, a mannerism, his smell -- something felt familiar. It wasn't until they were dancing the Polonaise, that Princess Caroline became aware of the role Prince Carlton had played in her kitchens only eight weeks prior. When she challenged him regarding his visit dressed as a servant, the Prince escorted her out to the balcony where they could have a somewhat private conversation.

Just as he suspected, she was first to speak. "You are quite the pretender sir! Servant indeed!"

Though she pretended to be annoyed, Carlton couldn't help but see the smile behind her words. "I never thought you would actually come. What changed your mind?"

"Truly, I had no intention of coming. However, I promised my mother that I would at least meet you before I rejected our betrothal."

"So we owe this honor to your mother then? We must be sure to thank Queen Lydia for her kindness." said the Prince with an ever so slight bow. He would have left her standing there, but he thought better of it -- it would annoy her more to have to spend the whole evening dancing with him. Besides, none of the courtiers interested him anymore.

In silence, the prince led her back to the dance floor and before he knew it they were dancing the Quadrille. Surprisingly enough, the evening flew by and they both appeared to be enjoying themselves. As Carlton led the Princess back to her parents, she stopped just before they were within hearing range. "Another reason I came, was to find out which report of you I should believe. The Courtier's gossip or the Minstrel's song?"

"Minstrel?" the Prince feigned ignorance.

"Yes, Minstrel. He sings of a handsome prince who is a mighty hunter, master horseman, good to the people and a lady's man."

"I must meet this minstrel and hear his tune."

The Princess gave Prince Carlton a slight curtsey and joined her parents. Looking back at Prince Carlton, with a menacing smile, she said, "Maybe I can arrange it."

Addressing the King and Queen of Breckridge Hall, King Stefen asked, "Before we retire, may we speak with you in the study?" Leading the way, King Stefen motioned for Carlton and Caroline to join them.

They were all seated except for King Stefen, who stood by the fireplace with his arm resting on the mantel as he gazed into the fire. "Your Highness" he said addressing Queen

Lydia. "I think it is time that we release your daughter from this arranged marriage. As you recall, it was Queen Hannah's suggestion that our children be betrothed. I will admit, given our past, I was in favor of the union. However, now that the children are grown, I feel it would be honorable to let them make their own choice in a companion. Our marriages, have turned out to be a blessing. This I believe happened because all four of us chose to make it so. Let us give our children the freedom to choose."

Queen Lydia and King Markus looked deeply into each other's eyes. The King smiled and nodded. It was obvious that they had also discussed cancelling the betrothal. Queen Lydia then turned to King Stefen and said, "Your Majesty, we will release them from this agreement, if they will take the opportunity to get to know each other. Regardless of whether they marry or not, our Kingdoms have been allies for centuries and it is important that this feeling of respect and peace carry on through the next generations."

"Agreed!" said King Stefen as he gently kissed Queen Lydia's hand. King Markus got to his feet and the monarchs shook hands.

Prince Carlton, sat in amazement. *After all these years, the freedom to choose?*

Princess Caroline must have been experiencing the same feelings. They both sat in silent bewilderment.

Princess Caroline was the first to speak. "Father? Mother? Before I honor this agreement I feel it is necessary that I know all of the facts. Clearly there was a reason for this betrothal and now the release? Why the secrecy? Please tell me."

King Markus gave Princess Caroline a slight nod and smiled at King Stefen. "I believe they are entitled to know, do you want to tell them privately or shall I rehearse our courtships here and now?"

After a few moments of awkward silence, Queen Hannah stood. "May I tell it?" This was a little surprising, but seemed acceptable to both monarchs.

The Queen beckoned the young couple to come sit on a settee nearer so that she could speak using her soft voice. "A tale such as this should be told with much tenderness."

The three couples sat close and comfortably as they prepared for the new revelation about to be passed on.

This turn of events seemed strange to Carlton but certainly not unpleasant. Admittedly, he had never been much for love stories or romance. However, these past eight weeks he had not only been watching his father, but he notice his mother as well. He admired the support and strength that she added to the Kingdom and especially to his family. She had always been a good loving mother, but he had just began noticing that she was not just physically beautiful, but that she had an inner beauty and strength that he admired and respected. He had always felt the love his parents had for each other and naturally just assumed that he too would have that type of a marriage one day.

As Queen Hannah began to tell their story, both monarchs took their wife's hand and held it tenderly to their lips.

"Many years ago, 30 to be exact, your father, Carlton, King Stefen, and your Mother," she said looking at Caroline, "Queen Lydia, were silently betrothed. Lydia was born here in Cantwell of royal blood and certainly a good match for the King. They had fallen in love and the Kingdom would truly have been blessed by their union.

Just then Queen Lydia interrupted, "Oh, Hannah, may I?"

"Of course," said Queen Hannah with a smile.

"I had been promised by my father to King Markus when I was but a child, much the same as you Caroline. However, I was not aware of this arrangement and neither was Stefen as he too was just a young man. Our two Kingdoms had enjoyed peace for many decades.

"When Markus learned of my affections for Stefen, he graciously absolved his prior claim. His parents had passed on and we had never met. He was, as you can imagine, quite sought after himself, like you Prince Carlton. Markus was happy to make his own choice in a companion. So it seemed our sordid triangle was going to end to everyone's satisfaction.

"Preparations were made for our wedding and announcements sent to all of the neighboring Kingdoms.

There was an air in the Kingdom that sang of peace and pleasure. Everyone shared in our joy."

Obviously shocked by this revelation, the Prince interrupted, "What happened?"

"King Markus planned to attend the wedding to show his support and continued friendship with our Kingdom. As he travelled to the wedding, he passed a traveling minstrel. He paid him for a song and that song changed all of our lives."

King Markus laughed, "I should have paid him more. I would have, too, if I had known what a difference it would make in our lives." He gently kissed Lydia's hand and smiled.

Raising her voice slightly, Princess Caroline asked, "What could the minstrel possibly have said to end a wedding of two who were in love?"

The monarchs looked at each other hesitantly.

"Do any of you remember the song?" asked Carlton.

"Trust me son, none of us will ever forget that minstrel's song. It changed our lives." replied King Markus.

"It united all of us forever." confessed King Stefen.

In unison the two monarchs repeated the words of the minstrel song.

"King Norman of Ravenswood celebrates tonight.

For he gains a Kingdom without a fight.

A betrothal dissolved, to another she'll wed

An alliance, formed through the marriage bed.

No matter how he fights none can come to his aid

For if he marry Lydia the Kingdom he can't save."

Now King Stefen stood and began pacing. "You see, Cantwell law states that no King or Prince for that matter can remain on the throne if they marry local nobility. This was a law that was written when Ravenswood and Cantwell Kingdoms were divided. We believe it was instituted to keep the Kingdoms united as much as possible, forcing them to marry from neighboring Kingdoms. It had been several generations since we have had much at all to do with the Ravenswood Kingdom.

"We were unaware of this law. If I had married Lydia the two Kingdoms would become one Kingdom and our family would be left desolate. King Norman would become heir.

"Lydia and I believed we could live as paupers, but we knew we should consider the Kingdom as well. We did not know what kind of a ruler King Norman was and how he would treat our people.

"King Markus generously suggested that he marry Princess Lydia, as originally arranged by her father. The arrangement must have been made to protect the people and kingdoms. This way she could still be close to the kingdom and the friends that she had grown to love."

Now Queen Lydia began to speak. "Broken hearted, Stefen felt he would never find another love. He asked me to choose a wife for him from Breckridge. Hannah and I have been friends for most of our lives."

"This is how it began." interrupted Hannah, "however, on our wedding day the four of us made a vow. We would never look back at lost love, but only to the future with our new spouses and make sure that they became the love of our lives."

Speaking for the others, King Stefen said, "We have all been truly blessed in our marriages and none of us would change the outcome." The monarchs gazed into their wife's eyes and love filled the silent room.

"When you were born Caroline, Hannah suggested that the two of you marry. Thinking of our two kingdoms united forever, pleased us all," said King Markus.

Hannah looked up and took Carlton's hand. "I know it sounds selfish, but it was the only way I felt I could right the wrong that had been done."

King Markus broke the silence. "It is because of the love we have found and worked at, that we want you Carlton and you, Caroline, to find the same love and joy in matrimony."

"Therefore, as your parents, we ask that you take the time to get to know each other. If after six months of courtship either one of you desire to dissolve your betrothal, we will support you wholeheartedly.

Carlton was overwhelmed by the whole affair. He wanted to go hunting to clear his mind. A few months ago, that is exactly what he would have done. Now he felt more of an obligation to King and country.

Caroline also felt it was a lot to take in, but the young couple agreed to their proposal and left the study.

Part 5

Queen Lydia, King Markus and Prince Everett left the following day. Carlton fully expected Princess Caroline to leave with them. However, Caroline accepted King Stefen's invitation to stay for a fortnight. She and her companion or lady-in-waiting, would be their guests, allowing Prince Carlton an opportunity to win her, if he should choose.

Learning that the princess had decided to stay, pleased Carlton. Whether it was the challenge to make her like him or the fact that she was more interesting than any other woman he had ever met he was not sure. No matter the reason, he needed a plan. What kinds of things would Princess Caroline enjoy doing? Carlton hurried to the breakfast room, hoping to find his mother alone. He was certain that she would have some ideas.

As he entered the room, he tried not to let his disappointment show. There sitting next to his mother, was Caroline. Queen Hannah smiled knowingly and greeted him. "Oh there you are Carlton! I was just telling Caroline that you wanted to show her our private gardens. She seems to enjoy flowers just as her mother and I do."

Carlton kissed his mother on the cheek and sat next to her. Why hadn't he thought of the gardens? Women seem to really enjoy flowers. He often found his mother in the conservatory or sitting on a bench in her private gardens.

Then the thought struck him, *Why was Caroline up so early? I don't know a single courtier who is up before ten.*

"Would you mind showing me the gardens, Prince Carlton?" Caroline seemed genuinely interested.

"Of course, I'd be honored. Please call me Carlton, I think it will be much easier."

"If you like, you may call me Caroline."

"Thank you," said the Prince with a slight bow.

Soon Matilda entered with a few kitchen maids each bringing a plate of breakfast. That is when it occurred to Carlton that his father was not with them.

"Where is father?" he asked the Queen.

"He will join us shortly. We've had another visitor from Ravenswood, requesting an audience."

"Where is Ravenswood?" asked Caroline. "I have never heard of it"

"I am not surprised that you are unfamiliar with that Kingdom. It is a good three days ride south of here. They keep mostly to themselves. Every once in a while we receive a visitor as they are traveling through. Other than that we don't know much about them." said the Queen.

They had barely begun to eat when King Stefen entered the room. They all began to stand and King Stefen motioned them to stay seated. "Is everything ok, Father?"

King Stefen looked concerned, but quickly brushed it away and smiled. "Everything is fine. Matilda, I had Mason take the gentleman to the kitchens. Please see that he gets a meal and some provisions to take with him."

Matilda curtsied and quickly left the room.

"Stefen, are you sure everything is ok?" Hannah knew him all too well, she knew he was concerned about something.

"Yes, dear. I'm sorry, I just have a lot on my mind. Everything is fine. How did you sleep Caroline? What are your plans for the day?"

Caroline's face lit up as she told the King of their plans to see the gardens. "Mother says Queen Hannah has the most beautiful garden she has ever seen! I hope Carlton will take me there right after breakfast!"

"Of course, you will love the gardens, but make him take you to Hannah's private garden first. I must warn you though, seeing them first will make the other gardens pale."

Caroline seemed to be eating faster, finally she announced that she had eaten all the food she could handle. "May I please be excused to get a bonnet and my wrap?"

The King smiled and nodded his head. "Carlton, you'd better hurry up."

Now that Caroline had gone, Carlton asked, "What is going on with Ravenswood? Do you need my help?"

"No, son. Don't worry about it. Enjoy your time with the princess."

Although Carlton could sense the concern his father was trying to conceal, he was quite willing to let his father handle it. "The more I learn about your responsibilities, father, I am not anxious to become King."

"Not all of my affairs are as pleasant as taking a beautiful princess to your mother's gardens son, but as a King we are blessed with advisors and assistants. Enjoy the leisure while you can."

When Caroline returned, she had everything she might need. Her bonnet, gloves and a wrap. Carlton could not help but agree with his father. There is nothing better than spending time with a beautiful woman in the gardens, or wherever for that matter.

Carlton excused himself and offered his arm to Caroline. "If you need us, we will be in the maze." He winked at his mother.

With a look of confusion, Caroline said, "I was hoping to see your mother's gardens first."

"The maze is very beautiful, and probably my favorite! I insist that you humor me and see it first."

With obvious disappointment, Caroline agreed to see the maze first, if he promised to take her to the Queen's gardens right after.

"As you wish," he said with a mischievous bow. He enjoyed having the upper hand with the princess. She was making every effort to be accommodating and Carlton decided to take advantage of it because he knew it would not last long.

As soon as Caroline realized that the garden was only accessible through the maze, she would most likely chide him. But until then, he would enjoy it. He dismissed the fleeting notion to lose her in the maze as he didn't think she would see the humor in it.

Caroline continued to hold Carlton's arm until they reached the garden entrance. The Prince knew the maze so well that he could probably find the entrance in the dark. The entrance was completely covered in vines and unless you knew what you were looking for it appeared to be another dead end in the maze. Carlton hesitated for a few minutes wanting to see the obvious frustration on the princesses' face.

Pulling her arm away, Caroline turned to leave the maze. "Prince Carlton, if you don't want to take me to the gardens, I am sure that your mother will!"

Carlton chuckled, only making Caroline more frustrated. Just as she started walking away, Carlton spoke, "Caroline, wait. This is the entrance."

She turned, giving him a look that he hoped would not be the last of its kind. She obviously did not believe him. Though he enjoyed teasing her, he decided that Caroline had taken enough of his teasing for now.

Carlton quickly found the latch and swung the gate open. The rustling of the vines made Caroline stop and look. She quickly came to investigate.

"I have never heard of a garden inside of a maze."

Carlton held the gate and stepped aside so Caroline could enter the Queen's Garden.

She gasped as she stepped through the entry way. He gave her plenty of room as she stood wide eyed with her mouth partially open trying to take it all in.

The Prince sat on the bench just inside so he could relax as Caroline scanned the garden, trying to take in what she saw as she looked at all of the plants and flowers. *What is it about flowers and women?*

After Caroline had thoroughly surveyed the garden several times, she came and sat next to Carlton. "Mother told me about this garden and I tried to envision it. Her description did not do it justice. Of course, there are some things that just can't be described, only experienced."

The princess seemed completely overwhelmed by the beauty of the gardens. As Carlton looked around, he only saw flowers, some in bloom, and some yet to bloom and others that had already blossomed. To him the garden was a peaceful place to sit, but its real wonder was the hold it had over his mother and now Caroline. *Do all women actually enjoy flowers this much*?

Carlton was ready to press on and show her the public gardens, he stood and went to offer her his hand and thought better of it. Somehow, Caroline was still mesmerized.

Seeing his mother's shears on the table he picked them up and looked for a flower that would match Caroline's outfit. Finally, he settled on a pink camellia. He cut it so she could carry it in her hand or fasten it on her dress through a button hole. The Prince then stood before her with his hands behind his back. Bowing ever so slightly he said, "My Lady, would you accept a small token from a lowly servant?" He sheepishly gave her the camellia.

Caroline, accepted the flower and smiled at Carlton. *Could he really be this charming? A pink camellia? That means "longing for you".* *Does Prince Carlton understand flowers!* She had never met a man that could understand the meaning of flowers. That is more than she could have ever hoped for in a suitor. *Is he trying to tell me that he has already decided he wants to honor our betrothal?*

I will be open minded, but I will not be so hasty. After all, this decision is for a lifetime! They spent the rest of the morning walking through the gardens around the castle.

They took afternoon tea on the patio with King Stefen and Queen Hannah. Queen Hannah noticed the camellia on the Princesses dress. It reminded her that she should speak with Carlton privately. Seeing her recognition, Carlton said, "Mother I hope that you don't mind me clipping a flower out of your gardens?"

Hannah nodded her approval and smiled. She knew that the Prince had no idea what a camellia would mean to Caroline. No doubt, Lydia would have taught her lovely daughter the language of flowers.

"Have you seen enough gardens today?" asked the King.

"Oh, I believe I could be entertained all day in your lovely gardens, but I think Prince Carlton is ready for a change," she said with a smile. "May I see your stables this afternoon?"

The King smiled and tipped his head toward Carlton. "I am sure Carlton would love to show them to you. One of these days I will have him show them to me as well. It has been several years since I had much of anything to do with them."

Carlton was pleased with her interest. "Do you ride? The countryside is magnificent this time of year. The farmers are preparing for harvest and the patchwork is a wonder to see."

King Stefen quickly interjected, "Carlton, take her in an open carriage. That is truly the best way to see the countryside!"

Seeing the look of panic and fear in Queen Hannah's eyes, Caroline said, "Thank you, I believe that would be perfect!"

"It's settled then, we are off to the stables." Carlton stood and led Caroline in the direction of the Royal Mews.

"They make a lovely couple, don't they Stefen?" Hannah said with a smile.

"I believe they could make each other very happy, if they choose to." He smiled and winked at his wife.

"Stefen, was the visitor from Ravenswood in need of anything? Is everything alright?"

"I confess, Hannah, I am still not sure what to make of it. He said he was a servant in the castle and that he felt a need to leave to secure the safety of his family. It's been a while since I have visited Ravenswood. I will look into the matter."

"Oh Stefen, don't go alone, can't you send a few of the guards? They don't have to be threatening."

"We won't go announced, Hannah, don't worry."

Part 6

The royal mews were in prime condition. The Master of the Horse, took his job seriously and insisted that all of the stable hands take great pride in what they did. The horses were, of course, well-groomed and their stables immaculate.

Carlton asked them to prepare the carriage while Caroline visited many of the stalls. "So, do you ride?" asked Carlton. "You seem to love the animals."

"Mother always forbade it, she said that riding side saddle is dangerous."

"And you have never tried it? This from the princess that works in the kitchen?"

Caroline smiled and said, "I guess you can call that our compromise. I desperately wanted to ride and mother knew my desire to cook as well. So, she arranged for me to have the privacy of the kitchen for an hour or so a few times a week and I promised not to ride a horse."

"What does she have against horses?"

"That was the rest of the compromise. I was to accept her terms without question."

"So, when was this unique settlement?"

"Well…I guess I was about eight years old, so twelve years ago."

"Twelve years, that is amazing! Was it an arrangement for life?"

Caroline looked thoughtfully, "I suppose it was not a lifelong arrangement. I am of age now, and here I am with a remarkable equestrian. Would you teach me to ride, Prince Carlton?"

"Are you sure? What about your mother's wishes?"

"Well, I believe her major concern was riding side saddle. But she also felt I was too young. I am older and taller now and I have a master teacher! With the proper gear, I can ride astride. I don't see how she can object!"

Just then the driver approached and was acknowledged, "Your carriage is ready, Your Highness."

"Thank you Jenkins, Caroline?" Carlton offered his arm and led her to the open carriage. "This is a much safer way to ride and allows us the opportunity to visit."

Caroline seemed to enjoy the carriage ride almost as much as the gardens. They both spoke openly and comfortably. It was as if they had always been friends.

"You were not teasing when you said how beautiful the countryside is this time of year! I have never taken the opportunity to view the country side or villages in my own Kingdom. I felt it would be easier to keep my promise not to ride a horse if I didn't know what I was missing."

Carlton looked out at the countryside. "If you agree, I will teach you to ride, Caroline. This is beautiful, as you have indicated; however, there is an added beauty when you experience it mounted on a horse."

Sensing his sincerity, Caroline said, "Then I shall not be satisfied until I have learned to ride! May we begin tomorrow?"

"Why not? I must confide in you, I have never taught a princess how to ride, but I will be pleased to teach you as much as you are willing to learn."

Time passed quickly – they shared the frustrations and limitations of being royal, recognizing the imbalance it placed on them in making decisions and the unfair judgements that could come about because of their lives and privileges.

They also shared awkward times. Carlton reflected on a hunting trip. He had been so focused on the fox he neglected to watch where he was riding. Suddenly, he found himself flat on his back. When he opened his eyes, he saw about ten servants staring down at him. He could feel their laughter, even though it was completely silent.

Caroline confessed that even though she had studied diligently and received excellent marks, it took quite a bit of diplomacy by the King to repair the damage when she confused her verbs while talking to a foreign dignitary- she committed to take her study of languages more seriously.

They had tea in one of Carlton's favorite spots that was reachable by carriage. It was evident that his mother and the kitchen staff went to a lot of trouble as they saw the "banquet" spread before them.

Carlton couldn't resist, "Tell me, Princess, how do our cooks compare to your cooking? Any tips you would like me to pass on?"

Unable to leave it alone, Caroline replied, "Sometimes it is not so much about the recipe or the ingredients, but rather the attitude of the one eating the meal."

Carlton felt like he had fallen off his horse again. He had enjoyed Caroline's biscuits, but now was *not* the time to tell her.

They walked around the meadow and Caroline pointed out the herbs and flowers that were plentiful and pleasant – at least to her. Carlton was more interested in the movement of a bush and the wildlife in the area, but enjoyed seeing her excitement as she listed the various plants. When she seemed to tire, Carlton assisted her back into the coach and smiled. He was pleased with the events of the day.

They sat in silence for a few minutes, taking in the beautiful sunset, a touch of pink nestled in the billowing clouds.

"Red at night, sailor's delight" she whispered.

"You're right, it's getting late. Jenkins, we'd better head for home."

The driver tipped his head in acknowledgement and turned the team toward the castle.

"It has been such a beautiful day Carlton, thank you."

"I will tell Matilda to get you some riding clothes for tomorrow morning, if that suits you?"

"Yes, that would be lovely, thank you. My lady-in-waiting is young and very inexperienced, I would like to keep it from her as well. Would Matilda be willing to help me dress?"

"Of course, are you sure you want to learn to ride? I don't want Queen Lydia to be angry with me. I wouldn't like to upset -- your mother."

"I am sure it will be fine, but can we keep it from our parents until I see my mother in person? I think it would be best to tell her myself."

"Absolutely! I will tell the servants not to mention it to anyone."

Caroline's smile gave a hint of concern and excitement. "I can't believe I am finally going to ride a horse!"

Carlton couldn't help but feel her anxiety and enthusiasm. He did love horses and if he and Caroline were going to spend time together he would like a good portion of the time spent riding in the countryside.

Carlton had the coachman take them straight to the castle. They were having guests to dinner who would be arriving within the hour. He knew that Caroline would want time to freshen up before they arrived.

He wondering how Caroline would dress for this dinner party. No one would be dressed as formally as they had been for the ball, but Carlton was anxious to see Caroline in another beautiful dress. He admired her choice in fashion and appreciated it when the women at court were clothed modestly. To him, it demonstrates a great deal of respect and makes everyone present feel at ease. Especially when dancing.

Carlton had just entered the great room when Caroline began descending the stairs. The Prince was situated in such a way that the door frame hid him from view of the princess, but allowed him to see her completely. Her eyes shone a brighter blue because of her beautiful pale blue dress. Her long brown hair was pulled back in a loose bun with several ringlets neatly arranged at the base of her neck.

Carlton hid behind the cover of the door frame as long as he dared. His mind was racing. Not only was Princess Caroline beautiful, but she had a personality to match. The short time that had passed since the ball, had been, in Carlton's view, wonderful. Had he known what an amazing person Caroline was, he never would have complained about their betrothal.

The day fly by so quickly. If the rest of her stay was like today, in no time she would be returning to her Kingdom.

He knew what he wanted, but was six months enough time to convince her that he was the Prince for her?

Dinner went smoothly, Caroline was intently watching the courtier's swoon over Prince Carlton. All she could do was shake her head in disgust. If it had not been for his obvious look of annoyance, Caroline would have excused herself and gone to bed early. She had truly enjoyed every minute she had spent with the Prince.

After dinner, the courtiers took turns exhibiting their musical skills. *Is it my attitude or are they really that desperate to capture Carlton's attention?* Some played the harp and others sang…love songs, *yes love songs – where is their sense of propriety?* Caroline was annoyed.

Carlton was very much the gentleman and applauded after each song, but Caroline could see the frustration in his face. Finally, after almost all of the courtiers had performed, Carlton interrupted. "Caroline, I have heard that you play the harp, could we impose upon you to play for us?"

Caroline rarely played for large gatherings, but for some reason she wanted to perform for him. "It's been such a lovely day, I would appear ungrateful if I refused. Have you a favorite song you would like me to play?"

Queen Hannah interjected, "Caroline, do you by any chance know *The Garden Path*? It has always been one of our favorites."

Caroline smiled as she placed her fingers on the harp and pulled it down to rest on her shoulder. "That is also one of my favorites!"

As Caroline played the beautiful tune, Carlton noticed for the first time how attractive a woman could look seated at the harp. She seemed to glow as she plucked the strings. He recognized the song as one that his mother often hummed when she thought she was alone.

All too soon the melody was over. Queen Hannah, with tear filled eyes, whispered, "Thank you."

Caroline had played so well, that none of the courtiers were willing to follow her. That suited Carlton, he wanted to keep that picture and tune in his mind as he retired for the evening.

King Stefen must have felt the same, because shortly after Caroline finished playing he stood and offered his arm to his wife. Following his lead, Carlton stood and escorted Caroline back to her room.

Caroline woke early the next morning with a smile of great anticipation. She was more than eager to begin her riding lessons. As she began to dress, she chose a simple frock. Prince Carlton would have some special clothes set aside for her for today's lessons.

Clara, her lady-in-waiting, said, "Your Highness, Prince Carlton sent you a parchment."

She handed her a note folded in half, accompanied with a carnation and a pink ribbon. Smiling, Caroline gently untied the ribbon and after smelling the beautiful carnation she read the note.

Caroline,

We have a change in plans today. Please forgive me and accept my invitation to accompany me on a carriage ride after breakfast. It will take the better part of the day as I want to share with you some of the beautiful countryside and people in our Kingdom.

If you will accompany me we will have a picnic lunch with a view such as you have never before seen!

Please accept my apology for the change in plans and my assurance that we will do what we had planned for today, tomorrow!

Yours,

Carlton

She was disappointed not to begin riding lessons today, but she was excited to spend another day with Prince Carlton. And he sent a carnation! *Can he truly love me?*

Caroline hurriedly dressed, she placed the gifted ribbon in her hair and hurried to the breakfast room excited to see what Prince Carlton had in store for her.

The King was absent at breakfast, but Queen Hannah seemed especially happy today.

"Caroline, I do hope that you will forgive the change in plans. Carlton tells me you had made some plans for today, but I asked him to take you to a favorite place of mine. Other than my gardens this holds a special place in my heart."

Carlton looked at the Princess apologetically. "Mother suggested that we join them today and we can do as we had planned tomorrow."

"The King is off on business this morning but I persuaded him to join us this afternoon. I do hope you don't mind.

"As you may recall, I too am from Breckridge Hall. Whenever I get homesick, I have Stefen take me to this place. You will understand when you see it."

Caroline was not surprised that Queen Hannah and her mother were such good friends. They were so much alike. Caroline knew she could never refuse Queen Hannah any wish if it was within her power. "If it is a special place to you, I shall not rest until I see it!"

The Queen seemed pleased and resumed her duties of seeing to the servants and their daily instructions.

Carlton grimaced as he realized again, that to this point in his life, he had been focusing on all of the wrong characteristics in himself, his choice of friends and companions. The beauty that he saw in his mother and now in Princess Caroline, could not be purchased with gold or jewels. The question now became, did he possess the qualities that it would take to win such a woman? Would she be willing to let him try, to work with him?

The air was cool, but pleasant as they rode in the open carriage. Carlton found himself being a spectator most of the morning as Queen Hannah and Princess Caroline talked and laughed sharing stories of Breckridge Hall, past and present. Surprisingly enough, he didn't mind. He enjoyed seeing his mother so happy and at ease with Caroline.

Up to this point, it seemed that neither of the women had spent much time looking at the countryside. However, as the team began to pull at a slower steady climb, they looked around. In the distance they saw King Stefen with another carriage and not far from it stood a blue canopy. Underneath the canopy sat a table and chairs set for four. To the commoner, it might look out of place, but to the Prince it was his mother's handiwork. There on the center of the table was a beautiful bouquet. Nothing left undone.

With my mother's help, Carlton thought, *I just might win Caroline's heart!*

Their luncheon consisted of a variety of small sandwiches with Carlton's favorite, cucumber and bacon. The fresh juices were especially welcome.

The King smiled knowingly at Carlton as he kissed his wife and lead her to her chair. "It's lovely Hannah! Have you told them why you chose this spot?"

"No dear, I was waiting until they saw it. Did you bring your spy glass?"

The King's Valet quickly handed him his spy glass. Taking off the cover and twisting it ever so slightly, the King handed it to Hannah.

Looking through the glass toward the East, the Queen smiled approvingly and handed the glass to Princess Caroline.

The Princess took the glass and looked at Carlton who let his shoulders rise and fall in an I-have-no-idea-fashion.

Placing the glass to one eye and looking in the same direction as the Queen, Caroline smiled and exclaimed, "Breckridge Hall!

"As young brides, your mother and I would ride here often. This was our special place. Now, whenever I get homesick for Breckridge, the Mountains or Lydia, Stefen brings me here."

Princess Caroline handed the spy glass to Carlton and took Queen Hannah's hands. "Thank you for sharing this with me. Ever since we met, just a few short days ago, it became obvious to me why you and my mother are such dear friends. Thank you!"

Surprised at all of the emotion in the air, Carlton looked through the glass at Breckridge Hall as if for the first time. Never in his life had he coveted anything belonging to another Kingdom until now. Presently, Breckridge Hall held the heart of the woman he wanted to win. In spite of all the times he had brought his mother to this ridge, he hadn't grasped the significance of the view.

After a lovely tea, King Stefen and Queen Hannah left in their coach giving the young couple some time to themselves, if they should choose.

The servants cleared the picnic sight and Carlton asked Caroline about Breckridge Hall. She began in her jesting manner to expound on the qualities of her home. "As you can see, young man, the majestic mountains need no ceremony. Their beauty is there for all to see, however had you spent more time in our Kingdom, you would have met a people, genuine people, who love and serve their King! Much like yours, I imagine," she said with no jest. "It is much colder there, but tradition has it that our Kingdom is notable for their beautiful seasons, rich heritage and traveling minstrels."

Then with that teasing gleam in her eyes she said, "You know, that first time you came to our kitchens, I would have sworn that you were a minstrel. Until I heard you speak that is!" With a laugh she snatched the spy glass and began surveying the rest of the view. "Let's see what else is out there."

As she took one last look at the beautiful view, her eyes caught hold of a section of land far away that looked desolate. "Carlton, what is that? What happened there?"

As Carlton joined her, he surveyed the valley. "I believe that is Ravenswood Kingdom."

"Does anyone live there?"

"Yes, my father occasionally speaks of visitors from there. Remember the other morning at breakfast?"

"What happened to their Kingdom? Isn't that the King that would have inherited Cantwell if my mother had married your father?"

"Yes, I guess it is."

"Has it always looked like that?"

"I honestly don't know." said Carlton. "Other than a few occasional visitors, I never hear much about them. Unlike you, we are short on minstrels!"

With that, Carlton offered her his hand, "We'd better be getting back to the castle. Mother will be waiting tea."

Part 7

An eager student makes teaching fun, but working with Matilda was rough. It took a lot of convincing to get Matilda to provide riding clothes. She was more than hesitant. "Are you certain you want to teach her to ride? Have you spoken to your father about it?" When that didn't work, she began offering alternative activities. "Have you taken her to see the beautiful cliffs in Dayton?"

Carlton's threat to go to the Queen and borrow her riding clothes made Matilda almost panic. "No, no, Your Highness, I will get her something. Please, do not speak with the Queen!"

Carlton found her reaction somewhat strange, but dismissed it as an oddity of an elderly servant. She provided what he needed, eliminating the need to speak with his mother.

Caroline began the first morning by acquainting herself with the horses. After an hour of meeting each of the horses, she felt she really wanted to ride Ginger, the Queen's horse. Ginger was a beautiful mare with a steady spirit.

Carlton felt comfortable with her choice and instructed them to prepare the mare to be ridden. This particular horse was not one that Carlton rode because of her calm spirit. He preferred a more lively horse. However, he knew that each of his horses were ridden daily by the servants under the Master of the Horse. His command to prepare Ginger met with a look of shock.

"Stanton, what's the problem?" asked Prince Carlton. "Surely we have a saddle that will fit Ginger?"

"Of course, Your Highness, but what about her Majesty? Your mother?"

"What about her? She won't be riding today. I haven't seen her ride for years, in fact. She never comes to the mews. Why should she care if Princess Caroline rides her horse?"

"Whatever you say, Your Highness. We will have her saddled and ready soon. Can we please keep her close to the mews this morning until you or I have a chance to speak with the King?"

Carlton was willing to accept his terms, as he intended to keep inside the paddock for a few days until both he and Caroline felt comfortable.

After the horse was saddled, Carlton had Caroline began by holding the reigns and petting the horses jaw. She naturally spoke gently to the horse and soon Ginger and Caroline were acquainted. Caroline then led her around the paddock slowly. After about a half of an hour, Carlton asked if she had had enough for the day.

"You're teasing me right? We have only just begun! Before the day is through, I want to be riding this beautiful mare!"

"We have to take it slow if you want to become proficient at it. Anyone can just jump on a horse. But you said you wanted to experience true horsemanship! That takes time."

"I understand, Carlton," she said submissively. Caroline led the horse to where Carlton was standing and then stopped. "We, Ginger and I, have already made a connection. We both want to get out of this paddock and see the countryside! ...today!" With that she smiled and batted her eyelashes.

"Princess Caroline! Are you flirting with me?" Carlton chuckled. "What do you think Ginger? Shall we put her on your back and see if you truly have a connection?" Carlton paused as he pretended to listen to Ginger's opinion.

"Stanton, saddle Thunder!"

"Caroline, if you will lead Ginger over to the mounting block, we will see just how connected you are!" Carlton hoped he would not regret this.

Smiling from ear to ear, Caroline led the horse to the mounting block. Carlton showed the princess how to tie the reigns to the hitching post and then had her repeat it several times. When he was satisfied she could make a clove hitch, he let her step onto the block.

"Talk to her gently as you slowly mount the saddle. She will become familiar with your voice and your touch. After a little while, she will long for it. Horses, like people, can become attached. If you truly have made a connection with Ginger, it will become evident within the next few weeks."

Ginger gave Caroline very little resistance, it was almost as if she truly did want to get out of the paddock with Caroline. Stanton arrived with Thunder. Carlton mounted and led Ginger around in the paddock. After a few minutes, Carlton gave Caroline the reigns. She seemed to take to riding quickly and was able to use the reigns quite skillfully for a woman who had never ridden before.

"So, you were just teasing me. You do ride!"

"No, I don't."

"Truly? I have never seen anyone handle the reigns as you do, and especially on their first time."

"I told you I was obsessed! I wanted to ride so badly! I had the stable boys in so much trouble. My father finally forbade them to let me ride, but he didn't say anything about teaching me how to hold the reigns. I practiced every day as I watched them exercise the horses. I sat on a saddle and tied reigns to a post. My parents ignored it for a while, thinking that I would tire of it. However, I did not. That's why my mother finally agreed to allow me to spend time in the kitchens if I would quit going to the stables."

"So, you are not the novice that I thought you were! Maybe a short ride outside of the paddock would be permissible today."

Carlton didn't think it was possible for Caroline's eyes to light up any more than they already were. But somehow they did. He had to let her go for a ride.

"Open the gates, Stanton! It seems that we are going for a *short* ride." He looked determined at Caroline when he said *short*. He didn't want those eyes of hers asking for more than he felt he should give.

The Prince did not miss the look of fear on Stanton's face, but the servant obeyed.

With the gates open, Caroline anxiously guided Ginger to the beautiful, green hills behind the royal mews.

"We should probably stay a little closer to the castle on your first ride, Caroline," said the Prince with tender caution. "Since you have never officially ridden a horse, you will be sore tomorrow, we best make it a short ride."

"We must not be seen by your parents or their servants. Should we follow this path?"

"Those eyes again! However did your parents ever tell you no?"

Caroline remained silent, but looked at Carlton intently.

"Ok, but we will stop and walk our horses for a distance. Otherwise, we won't have to *tell* my parents, they will know by the way you walk because of the soreness you will experience tomorrow!"

They rode to the top of the hill where a beautiful tree stood. They dismounted and sat in the shade of an oak tree. They talked about their childhood adventures and dreams. The hillside was a beautiful green speckled with wild flowers. Remembering how much Caroline liked flowers, Carlton picked a small bouquet of forget-me-nots and sweet peas.

"You can gaze upon these tomorrow when you are too sore to ride again!" With a smile he handed her the reigns and gave her a lift up onto her horse. "What do you think, Ginger?"

Carlton put his foot in the stirrup and swung onto his own horse. *What made this outing more special than other outings I have taken with other women? What hold does this princess have upon me?* These feelings were new to him. He was usually confident when in the company of a woman, however, he felt unsteady with this new feeling with Caroline.

Caroline smiled and patted Ginger's neck. These flowers would join the others he had given her. They would be pressed in her book of poetry and sonnets. *A forget me not. Can he be sincere? Each of the flowers he has given me have been expressions of love and desire. Did he pick them on accident? Is he teasing me? What is he really trying to say?*

He treated me with kindness and respect. When he looks at me, it's not a look of lust, it is hard to describe. But I like the direction it is going. Yes, I will pursue this relationship a little further. Yet, Sweet Pea could also mean good-bye, is he teasing me?

The next month flew by too quickly. Each day was spent divided between the Royal Mews and the Queen's Gardens. Both the Prince and Princess seemed genuinely disappointed when the day appointed for Caroline's departure arrived.

Somehow they had managed to keep her riding a secret from the King and Queen, but Carlton knew it was only a matter of time. He planned to speak with his parents directly after Caroline's departure. He knew that after the time she had spent riding, she would never be satisfied to go back to the kitchens.

Riding and horses gets into your blood. At least that is how it was for Carlton. It seemed to be that way for Caroline also. He doubted she would be able to forget the whole thing and resume her life in Breckridge Hall. However, his father had been able to forget his interest in the mews, maybe the Princess could too.

The Prince could not remember a happier or more satisfying time than this past six weeks. He smiled as he remembered the satisfaction he had felt when he realized who Caroline was at the ball. He had taken great pleasure in their verbal sparring. Their relationship had changed so much since then, at least it had for him. She sat toying with her breakfast and his heart ached already.

Panic began to rise in his chest as he thought, *when will I see her again? Surely this cannot be the end?*

As if sensing his pain, his mother broke the silence, "Carlton, would you join me in the gardens while Caroline sees to the finishing touches of her packing?"

As usual, the gardens were beautifully peaceful. Queen Hannah sat on her bench and beckoned Carlton to join her. "What's the matter, son?"

The Prince could never hide anything from his mother. It amazed him how perceptive she was and how she could truly feel as he felt. They had always had a strong bond. Perhaps because he was an only child. Carlton had always felt a responsibility to be strong; at least to put on a strong front for everyone, especially his father, the King. But when he was alone with his mother, he could be himself and she always knew the right things to say. At times her counsel was hard for Carlton to accept- many times he did not. But through the years, he learned, as he suspected most children do, never take you mother's counsel lightly.

As he accepted her invitation to sit next to her, he took her hands in his. "Mother, I can't let her leave me. I have never known such joy and now such pain. What can I do?"

Her knowing smile seemed to calm some of his fears as he hopefully awaited her advice.

Queen Hannah smiled, kissed him on the cheek, then she quickly arose and taking her clippers she began quietly talking to herself and cutting flowers. "fern, maidenhair, aster, gardenia, heather, white and lavender, arbutus, primrose for sure! Rose buds…"

Carlton stood up, frustration evident. "Mother! I am serious, I just spoke from my heart and all you can do is cut flowers?"

Remembering that Carlton did not understand what she was doing, she stopped clipping and turned to face him. "I thought you may want to send her home with some flowers. You see, women, especially Princess Caroline will appreciate appropriate flowers for the journey home. They will whisper to her on her journey."

"Oh, yes!" Carlton, calmed down and realization spread on his face. "Perfect! I should have thought of that myself. I know she loves your gardens, thank you Mother."

"If you want to see her again, you need to make sure she understands that before she leaves. I have seen the way she looks at you, Carlton. I believe she does care for you, too. But you must let her know!" The Queen took a small white ribbon from her wrist and wrapped it around the flowers making the bouquet complete."

As Carlton took the flowers he asked, "How will this tell her that I love her and I want her to stay? It's just a bunch of flowers."

Hannah smiled at her son. "Trust me Carlton. These flowers will tell her that you feel you have a secret bond of love, these flowers are that symbol. They will tell her that you think she is more beautiful than anyone you have ever met, that you admire her and will always protect her. That she is the only one you will ever love. That you cannot imagine life without her."

"All of that in a bunch of flowers? I know she loves the gardens, but they aren't even her favorite color! Why not just this?" Carlton pointed to a beautiful chrysanthemum.

"Oh, no dear! Trust me! Give her this and you will hear from her the minute she gets home! You see, to a woman, flowers mean so much more. They are perfect replicas of life! The planting, the growth, the bloom, even the withering."

"Ok, Mother I don't understand it, but I will do it! I trust you, especially with regard to Caroline."

"You'd better go to her, the coach will be leaving shortly. And son, hand her the bouquet after you have helped her into the carriage. Then whisper good-bye as you kiss her hand. Carlton, make sure you stand there until the carriage is out of sight. Don't leave her to look back at an empty drive. You must stand there until she is no longer in view. Understand?"

"This is more complicated than learning to fence, mother. I hope it works!"

"As do I son, as do I."

Carlton hurried out of the gardens and found Caroline saying her goodbyes to Ginger and the other horses in the stable.

Keeping his present behind his back, he offered his left arm to Caroline as he escorted her to the front drive.

"Thank you for teaching me to ride, Carlton. It is as wonderful to ride as I had always imagined!"

"Do you think you will be able to ride at Breckridge Hall? When will you tell your parents?"

"I've been thinking about that, Mother is much better with surprises! Breckridge Hall will be hosting the Jousting Exhibition soon. I am of age to now, so I will be presenting the award to the winner. What if I do it saddled on Ginger? Do you think Queen Hannah will allow me to ride her? Will you come?"

"You have given this some thought, haven't you? I don't know why the Queen wouldn't allow you to ride her horse. I'll need to tell them that I taught you to ride, should I wait until after you return home?"

Seeing the look of confusion on her face, Carlton added. "They may not like the fact that I taught you to ride, knowing that your parents oppose it so strongly."

"You're right! Make it just as soon as you can after I leave! Then you can send me word and I can complete the plans for my surprise. You will come, won't you?"

Not wanting to appear too eager, Carlton assured her that he would come. Did she really want him to come, or was it just so she could ride Ginger, a horse with which she has become so familiar? Only time would tell, but it was a step in the right direction.

Reaching the drive the coachmen stood alert with the door open, waiting for the Princess to ascend. Her lady in waiting was already in the coach and all of her trunks were safely stored on the coach that followed behind.

Helping her into the carriage, he waited patiently for her to gather her skirts and set her hand bag down. He carefully handed her the bouquet and giving a slight bow, kissed her gloved hand. As he closed the door he whispered, "I'll see you soon!"

Caroline grabbed his hand as the door closed, handing him a cube of sugar.

"Thank you, Your Highness, never have I received such a treasured gift," he said mockingly.

"Silly, it's for Ginger! One a day, to remind her of me, she mustn't forget me."

With a smile only Caroline could bring to his face, Carlton pocketed the sugar, and watched obediently for the coach to drive out of view. However, they had only gone a short distance when the coach came to a stop. Confused Carlton went to the window where Princess Caroline held out her hand.

As he approached she handed him a folded parchment. "I promised at the Ball that I would tell you of the Minstrel sonnet. I have penned it as closely as I can remember. Then coloring slightly, she brushed his hand and whispered, "Please come to the tournament, even if you can't bring Ginger."

As she sat back in the coach, their eyes fixed on each other, Carlton closed the door, tapped the coach and told the coachman, "Drive on."

With no one to hear his comment, Carlton still said out loud. "Yes, my beautiful Princess, I will be there! Know this, I hope to win more than just a jousting tournament!" Carlton didn't move until all three coaches were no longer in view. "The only problem I have right now is how do I exist until the tournament?"

Remembering the parchment, Carlton unfolded it and began to read:

Our dear Prince Carlton, always on a horse.

Hunting & fencing & flirting, a dead end course.

But now that same young fop, has turned himself around.

He's helping his people live, He won't run the Kingdom aground.

He knows names, hopes and dreams, even helping in their schemes.

Yes He's getting old –the King I mean –

We've no need to worry, the Prince will reign well and just.

But the son needs a bride, The Kingdom calls it a must!

But wait – I've heard a tale – a betrothal silences his tongue.

He's committed to someone much too young.

They say she's pretty and polite, she may fill our need?

Carlton deserves the best – not someone with power greed.

She's on her way to meet him, we'll see if she's a match.

But if she's like the others we'll throw her in the patch.

We look for growth and peace, as well as other things.

We want a happy marriage for our hero in the wings!

Part 8

"Your Highness?"

"What is it, Stanton?"

"Pardon me Your Highness, but have you spoken with your father about Princess Caroline and Ginger?"

"No, I have not. I am sure that he won't mind. While she is mother's horse, mother has not been to the stables for years. Father gave me charge over the Mews nine years ago. I believe he will sanction my judgment. Though you are right, should I decide to give her to Caroline, I will speak to mother first. That would be the best way to handle it."

It seemed Stanton accepted the Prince's comments, without question. However he made no attempt to resume his duties after Carlton's obvious dismissal.

"Stanton, what is it? Why are you so concerned about Princess Caroline and Ginger? Do you believe that the Queen will be upset by my giving her horse away?"

"No, Your Highness, that is not the problem." Stanton waited for the Prince to invite him to continue explaining his concerns.

Becoming impatient, Prince Carlton gave him a nod, "What is it Stanton?"

Gathering his courage about him, Stanton continued, "It is not my place to rehearse the details of Her Majesty's past, your father would not be pleased. I must urge you to seek him out and tell him of your teaching the Princess to ride and her desire to continue riding."

"I don't see why this is so difficult, Stanton. Mother used to ride, Queen Lydia used to ride. It is not as if women riding is forbidden."

"Please, Your Highness, I beg of you- speak with the King."

Seeing his discomfort, Carlton, nodded. Stanton then resumed his duties as Master of the Horse.

Finding the King was not difficult. He was in his study going over a few parchments that had arrived earlier that morning with a courier from Ravenswood Castle. "Father, do you have a moment?"

Looking up, the King motioned for his son to sit in the chair opposite him. Tossing the parchments on the writing desk in front of him, he appeared grateful for a distraction from his concerns.

After a deep sigh, Carlton rehearsed his story. "Father, while Princess Caroline was here, I taught her to ride Ginger. I am considering giving her the horse as a gift. Mother hasn't ridden her for years and she is the steadiest horse in the stables. Stanton seemed to think that there might be a problem and asked that I speak with you before I speak with mother." There, he had satisfied Stanton's request.

When he saw the look on the King's face Carlton was caught completely off guard. He had literally turned grey, never had Carlton seen his father at a loss for words.

After composing himself, the King stood and rested his arm on the mantle behind him, as if he needed physical support to get his words out. "Carlton, would you join me in my cabinet?"

"Father, are you quite alright?"

"Let's continue this conversation in my cabinet."

Still confused by the secrecy, Carlton quietly followed his father to his private chambers. After the King closed and secured the door, he offered Carlton a seat. "Son, I am concerned that your actions will hurt your mother more than you can possibly imagine."

"I know that Ginger is her horse, I meant no disrespect. I have never seen mother venture near the stables. You're right, I should have asked her."

"No! Don't mention it to her or anyone." Carlton had never seen his father so upset.

"Perhaps I should have had Caroline speak with Mother before she left. They seem to have a bond. I will find the Princess a different horse."

Speaking much softer now, the Monarch sighed, "It's not the horse son. You should not have taught her to ride. Not here, not with our history."

"What history, father?"

"I was hoping that I would never have to relate this tragedy to anyone, let alone my own son."

"Father?"

"Years ago, twenty-one, to be exact. Your Mother and I were planning for the arrival of another child. We were so pleased with the news that we would be blessed with another baby. Hannah loved the stables. She spent many hours grooming the horses and riding. Whenever Lydia came for a visit they would ride to the hill where we took you and Caroline."

The King walked toward a portrait that was covered with a black cloth. Carlton was surprised that he had never noticed this particular painting before. Pulling the covering off, he revealed a beautiful painting of two women mounted on horses looking over the vista. It was obvious that they were of royal birth, as both women wore cloaks with their Kingdoms crests embroidered on the back.

"Mother and Queen Lydia?"

"Yes."

"Why the black covering?"

"On this particular day, I did not accompany them. The artist as well as four of our most trusted knights escorted them. You see, this painting was to be a gift for me from your mother.

"Something spooked their horses. Your mother's horse, Beauty bolted for the stables. They were riding side saddle and Hannah was not prepared. I saw her horse coming at a solid run toward the mews with no rider.

"I caught the horse and Stanton followed with a carriage. We found your mother nearly dead just a mile from the castle. The physicians did everything they could to save her and the baby. Obviously the baby did not survive. Though it was an accident, Hannah has never stopped grieving. She vowed she would never ride again.

"As you know, I gave her Ginger only a few years ago. I thought, because of her gentle spirit, your mother would consider riding again. She loved riding so much, but she could not. You see son, it hurt her to even speak of it. After I gave her the horse she kept to her room and went into mourning all over again. We can't put her through it. You have my permission to give the horse to Princess Caroline. It may be good to have it out of our stables, however, do not speak to your mother about any of this."

Carlton listened intently as King Stefen related his tale. The understanding broke across his face, he said, "That is why you quit coming to the mews, isn't it?"

"Yes, son. Your mother is not the only one who cannot bear to relive the past. I almost lost her. She is my life. One day you might understand just what that means, but for now, you will just have to respect our wishes."

"I must really be shallow. To think, I had no inkling of the whole affair."

"You were young, Carlton. The servants don't speak of it because of their love for the Queen and her tender feelings. It is as though it never happened. But it did and it doesn't take much to bring it all back."

"I understand father. Can you tell me, is this why Caroline's mother forbade her to ride as a child?"

"Yes, I am sure of it. Lydia and Hannah are the dearest of friends. Remember, Lydia was here when it happened. There was a time, I believe, Lydia blamed herself. Not that she could have done anything. She felt guilty when she had a child the following year."

"I don't know what to do. Caroline wants to surprise her parents at the jousting competition next month. I am certain that she is not aware of the accident. Perhaps I should warn her not to?"

"Well son, I don't know how Queen Lydia feels now, but I believe that the Princess needs to at least know of the circumstances prior to the contest so that she can decide for herself."

"Perhaps it would be reason enough to pay her a visit?"

The King chuckled, "So, that's what this is all about, you need an excuse to visit the lovely Princess Caroline!"

Carlton was quick to make a clarifying statement, "Father, I don't want to spoil our relationship over a horse. Caroline is more than just another pretty face. She has inner qualities that I have not seen in any of the courtiers. She is the only person that has ever dared question my actions openly. She requires me to look at life through different eyes. But it's more than that, it's difficult to explain."

Putting his hand on Carlton's shoulder, the King smiled. "She brings out the best in you and encourages you to become the man she deserves."

"Yes! That's it! How did you know?"

"That is what your mother does for me. Not only does she bring out the best in me, but she completes me. Go on, son! If you need an excuse for the visit, you can always go hunting afterwards."

Prince Carlton walked thoughtfully to the door, pausing just before he left, he said, "Father, thank you for everything! Thank you for marrying mother, for making her the love of your life, for being a father and a King that I can look up to! I will do my best to be a better son and heir."

Part 9

Thorndyke had all of their provisions ready, they would leave within the hour. Seeking out his mother, Carlton went to say good-bye. He found her in her parlor quietly embroidering a pillow covering. "I am about to leave mother, any last minute advise?"

Hannah smiled and patted the seat next to her. Carlton, hesitantly obeyed sitting next to his mother on the settee. While he enjoyed the special attention Hannah gave him, especially in the privacy of her rooms, he was anxious to be on his way. But this time, with new thought he recognized that, in many ways, he would always be her little boy. It used to bother him, in his teenage years, he wanted to be treated like a man. However, the more he came to know his mother, the more he appreciated the little acts of love that she showed him.

"I know you are anxious, Carlton. Just be the man she knows you are son. Any woman would be blessed to be singled out by such a man!"

"Mother, you are prejudiced!"

"I certainly hope so! Don't bring her any flowers, this time. They would not withstand the ride and it would definitely not bode well with the hunting expedition! Give Caroline and Queen Lydia my love, please and tell them we look forward to the upcoming competition with pleasure!"

Kissing her on the cheek, Carlton said his good-byes. Yes, he must warn Princess Caroline. She must not ride Ginger during the tournament. He could not bear the thought of doing something that would cause his mother pain in any way.

The ride to Breckridge Hall seemed to take longer than Carlton remembered. He was anxious to see Caroline and to learn if she had missed him as much as he had missed her. This time he could ride through the front gates as a guest instead of concealing himself as a servant, however, the closer he got to the castle, he thought better of it.

He had brought Ginger for Caroline, so they took both horses to the mews. Following his father's advice, he did not speak of it to his mother, but felt that even if Caroline could not ride right now, she could at least enjoy the company of the horse she had grown to love so quickly.

He didn't overlook the fact that giving her the horse would also win him points in his campaign to win her heart. At least he hoped it would demonstrate his commitment.

After the horses were seen to, he went to the kitchens, where he anticipated he would find Caroline. It was still early afternoon, and if he was lucky, a certain scullery maid would be making biscuits. Carlton put on his best smile when Princess Caroline answered the kitchen doors. "Oh, no you don't!" she said with a hint of laughter. "We are not accepting peddlers today."

"Peddler? I am not a peddler. Just a poor, hungry prince in search of a few morsels."

The smile on her face told Carlton everything he needed to know. She was glad to see him, if only just a little bit.

"To what do I owe this honor, Your Highness?" Caroline gave a pretty curtsey and a mocking nod of her head.

"I am on my way to hunt, just beyond your borders and I have some news you might find valuable."

"Oh, so you are not a peddler, but a minstrel?"

"There will be no sonnet here, but the message is better than a minstrel's, for it is genuine."

Caroline placed a platter of biscuits in front of the Prince and sat in the chair closest to him. "I am ready, minstrel. Sing!"

While Carlton was enjoyed their bantering, he knew he only had a few minutes before the King and Queen would be aware of his visit. He quickly told Caroline about the accident his mother had while riding a horse.

"I am sorry, Caroline, but I believe that both of our mothers would experience more than shock if you were to ride out on Ginger for the jousting competition."

"I am sure you are right. I don't want to wound either of them. I won't ride at the competition, but I will need to tell my mother. I do not want to give up riding. I have missed our daily rides and all of the time spent with the horses."

Then with a bow, he handed her a sack of sugar cubes and a curry. "She is yours- if you still want her," he said with a wink and a half smile. "I thought that you might enjoy visiting Ginger everyday instead of just dreaming about her."

"She is here?" It took Caroline a few minutes to speak. Then with tears in her eyes she whispered, "Thank you! I have longed for our afternoon rides."

Her smile and the gleam in her eyes were enough for Carlton. This is why he had come. It amazed him how a simple smile could mean so much.

"I am sorry that you won't be able to ride her today, but we will find a way to break the news to our mothers soon. I promise."

Throwing her apron aside, Caroline grabbed his hand and headed toward the mews. After a proper greeting between Caroline and Ginger, they curried the horse in silence.

Not wanting to slight the King and Queen, Carlton offered Caroline his arm and they walked in silence to the castle. Prince Carlton noted that he felt completely comfortable in their silence. Especially when he knew she appreciated his offering of a horse. Never before had he given such a gift to a woman. For that matter, he had never met a woman like Caroline. He felt that there was nothing that he could ever deny her. He would give her the moon if it was within his power. Anything would be worth the sacrifice, just to see her smile as she just had.

Carlton reflected on the men he knew who fell captive to just one woman. He had no patience for them. Now he was one of them and began to understand why they fell. Oh the time he had wasted, playing the fop. He knew that there was only one woman for him, and she was holding the crook of his arm with both of her small hands as they walked through the gardens. Yes, he would give anything to have her care for him even a portion of what he felt for her.

Smiling at her, Carlton cupped her chin in his hands. "We will ride again, you will just have to wait until the timing is right. I will help you!"

"Come with me through the gardens and then I will take you to see my parents. They will be pleased to see you and even more pleased to know that we are together."

Carlton could easily be persuaded to abandon the hunting trip and spend more time with Caroline. *If only she would ask*, he thought.

Just as he suspected, to him, the gardens were every bit as beautiful as his mothers were. Like Queen Hannah's gardens, Queen Lydia's gardens also boasted of a large variety of flowers in all shapes and sizes. After a quick tour, Princess Caroline took his arm and led him into the castle. They found the Queen taking afternoon tea in the afternoon room. Ringing for the servants, she had them inform the King of Prince Carlton's presence and instructed them to bring refreshments for the four of them in the conservatory.

Carlton felt so at ease, he didn't want it to end. *If I only knew what Princess Caroline is thinking? Would she consider me as a suitor? She did say she enjoyed riding with me. However, she would most likely enjoy riding with anyone who would let her mount a horse.*

Not wanting to wear out his welcome, and unsure of Caroline's commitment or interest, Carlton bade them farewell shortly after they finished their refreshments. "May I walk you out?" asked Caroline.

"Yes, I would like that!"

"What color will you wear for the jousting competition?"

"I thought you didn't like a man who dresses nice. I believe you called me a fop?"

Smiling she asked again, "What color will your coat be? If I should ask you to wear my scarf for the competition, I would like it to match. I mean, knowing how particular you are about your apparel."

Thorndyke was waiting for him in the front of the castle. "I haven't decided on a particular jacket yet. What color is your favorite scarf? I will wear a coat to match it."

"Pink", she said with a menacing smile.

"Good! Pink it is!" He mounted his horse and walked to the gate. Remembering the counsel his mother gave him when Caroline left Cantwell, he turned and waved to the Princess with his cap. Then muttering to himself he said. "I don't wear pink my lovely, but I can certainly wear something handsome that will make your pink scarf stand out!"

Carlton was leaving the castle grounds when he saw Prince Everett riding toward him in a steady, determined stride. "Carlton! Can you spare a minute?"

"Certainly, Everett, what is on your mind?"

"What do you know of the Ravenswood Kingdom?"

"Very little, I confess. I know that my father has had many dealings with them. But I, myself, can tell you very little, is something bothering you?"

"There is a man here that I would like you to meet. Do you have a minute?"

"Of course!

Prince Everett turned his horse and led the way. "He is not far, only a short ride."

Riding toward a quaint cottage, Carlton noticed a small gathering of people. Most of them were peasants. As they neared the cottage, they could hear the lively tunes of a mandolin and laughter. Carlton caught up with Prince Everett and asked, "You brought me to hear a minstrel?"

Laughing, Everett slapped Carlton on the back, "Not just any minstrel, but Ravenswood's Minstrel! I do not generally listen to such tales, but this man spins a good one. I want your opinion. There may be merit to it."

It didn't take long for the small group to notice the approach of Prince Everett. Soon they all had knelt on one knee. The minstrel was the first to speak, taking the privilege of the entertainer. Standing and with a swirl of his colorful, feathered hat he bowed again asking, "To what do I owe this privilege, my Lord?" Then noticing Prince Carlton with his royal insignia, he repeated his bow and said, "Aye, not one Prince but two! 'Tis a marked day for me, to be sure!"

Following Prince Everett's lead, Carlton did not dismount his horse. Since this was Everett's kingdom and people, Carlton sat with anticipation.

Addressing the minstrel, Everett said, "I found your lively tune quite interesting and have invited my friend, Prince Carlton, to hear your tale. If you don't mind repeating it."

"Oh, Your Highness! I've many tunes that t'would interest the Prince far more than that one. What time have ye?"

Seeing that the minstrel was hoping for payment, the Prince smiled and tossed him a small purse of coins. "Just the song I asked for, you will find enough in the purse to not only continue your stay, but in comfort."

"Thank ye, m'lord." Bowing his head again he turned to a table on which he sat as he plucked at the mandolin. The crowd made themselves comfortable, either finding a place to sit or a tree to lean against.

Carlton had never really paid much attention to traveling minstrels. However, since his discovery of how his parents had met, he felt it would be wise to at least hear the tale. Princess Caroline apparently took occasion to hear their songs. Maybe Carlton should hear more of these colorful tunes.

Apparently ready for his performance, the Minstrel stood with the mandolin at his side, he addressed the gathering, "Tis the Prince of Ravenswood of whom I sing. A notable man, soon to be King!" Lifting his instrument, with a pleasant smile on his face he began his tune.

"Introducing, Prince Henry of Ravenswood, not as young as these lads", he said pointing a bony crooked finger at the two young princes.

Prince Henry is the up and coming king

The monarch of whom all minstrels will sing

He mastered all skills – though he was sheltered from his youth

All kingdoms are invited to see him demonstrate this truth

You ask about the ladies? He will not disappoint

He is handsome, charm oozes from each and every joint

Princess Caroline should not act in haste

'twould be sad her affections on another to waste.

His grandfather is passing Henry will be king

Queen of Ravenswood carries a nice ring

Take heed young princess of the man you adore

One skilled and prepared or, well another kingdom's boar.

The minstrel set down his mandolin, took off his hat and began circulating the crowd in hopes of receiving more coins. As he approached Prince Carlton, he said, "No offense intended, Your Highness." His hand open to receive payment.

"Minstrel, you've been more than paid for that tune!" Prince Everett gave the minstrel a warning nod. Then looking at Carlton he waited to see his reaction to this colorful tale. "Well, man? What do you think?"

Addressing the Minstrel, Carlton queried, "How old is this Prince Henry?"

In his theatrical way, the minstrel addressed Prince Carlton. "He be nearly threescore, Your Highness."

"Everett, I have never heard of this Prince, which is not to say he is not real. I will have to inquire regarding him." Then as an afterthought, Carlton asked, "Who have you invited to compete in the upcoming jousting festivities?"

"As usual, all of the neighboring Kingdoms. Ravenswood, however, has never chosen to participate."

"Well then," Carlton said addressing the minstrel again. "We shall see if this Prince Henry is all that you propose.

If he is not afraid to meet the challenge, we shall all have the pleasure of meeting him in less than a fortnight!"

As the princes rode away, the crowd began to gather around again and soon the minstrel was spinning another tale. Carlton thought he heard his name in a tune, and though he was curious, he knew it would not be appropriate for him to satisfy his curiosity under these circumstances.

When they reached the lane toward Breckridge Hall, Carlton said, "I will look into this Everett. I am sure that my father will know more concerning this Prince. Do you consider him a threat?"

"For the tournament? No. However, if he is soon to become King, I do think that both you and I should make time to get to know him. We have both enjoyed years of peace, I don't want to see that end. Especially if you should marry my sister!" With a jovial laugh Everett gave his horse a slight nudge and he rode off toward the castle.

Carlton did not mind the teasing. He knew that Everett was his ally in love and war. They rode toward the castle together. The two princes had always enjoyed their association and today was no different. As they reached the gate, they bid farewell, each going their separate way.

Prince Carlton cut his hunting trip short, due to lack of enthusiasm. All he could do was think of the Princess, and now the possibility of a rival, Prince Henry. Finding his father in his study, Carlton sat down. "Father, it's been so long since I have paid much attention to the jousting competitions. What does the winner receive? Will the princess bestow a kiss on him?"

"It's hard to say son, each Kingdom does it differently. Is that what you would like? A kiss from Princess Caroline?"

"I think it would be a perfect prize, if I am the winner. If I am not the winner, I would prefer them to receive a medal of some sort. A token to hand to them."

"Am I correct in my assumption? Are you fond of the Princess?"

"Of course I am fond of her, you know that! But how will I know if she returns my affections?"

"If she asks you to wear her scarf that would definitely be a sign that she is favoring you."

"What else? Surely there is something more!"

"How does she act when you are alone? Does she hold your arm? What about the silence?"

"Silence?"

"Yes, when you are alone is the silence uncomfortable?"

"No, I don't think so. There is never much silence, she is very talkative and so full of life!"

"Is there a competitor you are worried about?"

"I don't know. What can you tell me about Prince Henry from Ravenswood? Will he soon be King?"

"Yes son, he will. Is he, too, competing for the Princess Caroline's hand?"

"If the minstrel's tale is worthy of attention, Prince Henry intends to marry the Princess," Prince Carlton said with frustration.

King Stefen, pressed on, "His father, King Norman, married my Aunt, Lady Ivy. They were wed when I was but ten. In those days our Kingdom's were very much involved with each other. We held many of our festivities together.   After Lady Ivy's death in childbirth, our Kingdoms were officially divided. King Norman blamed the poor boy for his mother's death and he blamed my father for his sister- Lady Ivy's death."

"Why?"

"It's hard to say son, when you lose someone you love, there is never any reasoning to your actions. It appears that King Norman chose to turn to hate. That way he would never have to suffer again."

Carlton interrupted the King, "Father, he blames both child and brother for the same death? Is he mentally sound?"

"I am not sure of all of the details, but my father had always hoped for a reconciliation before his death. That never happened. For several years my father asked to see the boy and he was never allowed.   Markus and I became acquainted with him at school. His name is Broderick. He married a commoner and again, was a disappointment to the King. Prince Broderick's son Henry has been accepted by his grandfather and I believe that he has been sent

86

abroad until only recently- when his grandfather became ill and sent for him.

"I have heard conflicting reports about their Kingdom and I have sent couriers to send our concern and to gather what information they may. The last one has not returned home. Do you recall the visitor we had while Princess Caroline was here?"

"Yes, you had Matilda see to him after you had spoken with him. What did he have to say?"

"He told of a Kingdom in turmoil and sorrow. I cannot speak more of it until I am sure. A disgruntled servant can spin tales to suit their purposes."

"But you do think they may have some merit, otherwise you would not have sent couriers."

"True enough, son. However, I don't want to give false witness. If they are willing to become a part of our society again, I don't want to sway your opinion. At least not until any and all of my suspicions can be either confirmed or denied."

"Thank you father, that is wise. Where is Prince Broderick?"

"I don't know son, we lost contact with him after school. I only heard about his son because of my recent inquires.

"But enough of this somber topic!" With a teasing smile on his face, King Stefen asked, "Tell me about Princess

Caroline! When did you decide that you liked her? It wasn't because of her love of horses was it?"

Carlton did not dare tell him about the trip he had made to Breckridge Hall as a servant. Instead he replied, "She is very entertaining and stands up to me when she thinks I am in the wrong. Not many people have the courage to do that. I respect it and enjoy bantering with her. Is that bad?"

"That is not a bad way to begin a friendship. I believe to truly love someone, you must become friends first. Then when the hardships and trials come, your friendship will be able to support and sustain one another."

"Do you think Prince Henry will be a suitor I have to reckon with?"

"I don't know, son. I do know that you don't want to rush her into marriage and then always wonder if she had the time and opportunity if she would she have chosen someone else. If you love her, trust her to follow her heart. If she does love you, it will lead her into your arms."

"Now I know what mother saw in you! You are a romantic!"

The king shook his head and grinned, "Son, all I know about love, service and sacrifice I learned from your mother!"

The King stood, squeezed his son on the shoulder and walked out of the room. "Speaking of your mother, she is waiting tea for us."

Part 10

Finally the time had arrived for the tournament. Carlton bet the roads leading to Breckridge Hall were busy with travelers. This was the time when the Prince envied the commoners. They travelled in families mostly. Those who would compete with their own family and friends to root for them. They brought tents and provisions not only for the event, but for the journey as well. It was a more than a full day's journey from Cantwell Castle to Breckridge Hall. Carlton would spend the night at the Royal Lodge not far from Breckridge, but he sometimes wished he could spend the evening with the people.

As night fell, and they gathered around a fire, he heard music and laughter. *What would it be like? They seem to be happy and excited for the tournament, too.* Carlton decided he would also attend the Vespers Tourney. This tournament was held the night before the main event and it allowed the young men, nobles and peasants, a chance to compete. King Markus and King Stefen had always encouraged the winners of the Vespers Tourney to compete in the Jousting or Tilting Competition the following day.

Because Prince Carlton had become more involved in the daily lives of the people of his own Kingdom, he knew several young boys who had the skills and hopes of winning this tournament.

These same young men had come to Prince Carlton in the weeks prior to the tournament to ask for advice and to show their family coat of arms that they would be displaying during the Opening Day Procession.

The Prince knew that this was an event that all of the young men looked forward to each year. Some of the most notable knights in their history arose from these tournaments.

All that aside, he was not fooling himself. He knew that the real reason he had come early, was to spend more time with his beautiful Princess Caroline. At least he hoped she was his.

Before he left home his mother gave him a pink Camellia from her garden to put in his coat during the Procession. Then with a smile she said, "If you really want to win her heart, give her this flower after the procession."

"Thanks, Mother. I shall!"

Carlton had never had to work so hard to win a woman's attention. He was, however, not just seeking her attention, but her love and loyalty. Oh, how he missed her when she wasn't around.

When the Prince arrived at Breckridge Hall, he saw that tents and canopies of all colors and sizes were set up on the East side of the Castle Grounds. An air of excitement filled the whole Kingdom. It always amazed Carlton how these events tended to unite Kingdoms.

He, of course, would be staying in the guest wing of the Castle along with all of the other visiting gentry. Carlton did not linger too long on the lawns or in the gardens. He headed straight for the mews, he could have sent his horse with the servants as he normally would have done, but he thought Caroline may be there with Ginger.

Just as he had predicted,

Caroline was in the mews. They talked and when Carlton had finished unsaddling Thunder and seen to his needs, Caroline took his arm and they went to the private gardens. Carlton didn't care where they went as long as they were together.

Just as they were about to sit on a garden bench, Prince Everett and another gentleman came looking for them. "Prince Carlton, may I present His Highness, Prince Henry, of Ravenswood Kingdom."

While Carlton was anxious to meet him, he did *not* appreciate the timing. Nor did he like the way that Prince Henry was looking at Princess Caroline! Without missing a step, Carlton put his right hand on Caroline's hands so that she couldn't release her hold on his arm. He did not know if the minstrel was correct, but Carlton wanted Prince Henry to know that Caroline was his.

They exchanged pleasantries, and Everett suggested they join his father in the study and get to know each other better. This was the part of diplomacy that Carlton detested. He preferred to stay with Caroline, but it would be improper for him to refuse. If he suggested they meet in the library, they could include Caroline. However, the look on Prince Henry's face told him that any time he could keep Caroline from Prince Henry would be best. *What poor, poor timing – responsibility verses desire.* He nodded to Prince Everett.

Caroline knew that this invitation was for the men only and she slowly released her hold on Carlton's arm. With a smile she said, "I believe that Mother will be waiting for me in her bed chambers. She has been under the weather and I must take her tea."

"Please give her my best and tell her I hope to see her soon," said Carlton. Then in an effort to express his disappointment he took the Camilla from his coat and gave it to Caroline. He would have to get another for the procession. This seemed more pressing.

Not to be outdone, charm oozing from every word, Prince Henry said, "Yes, Princess Caroline, we will not be complete until both you and your mother are able to join us. I do hope that you will save a dance or two for me tonight?"

How dare he, thought Carlton, *What nerve! He is no Prince! He's a scoundrel!*

Caroline smiled at Carlton as if she could read his thoughts. "I would be honored to dance one waltz with you, sir. The rest of the evening is already taken."

Confused, Carlton looked at her with dismay. He had not had an opportunity to ask her for any dances and they were all gone? And her last with this knave?

Caroline excused herself and the Princes joined King Markus in his study.

"We have awaited your arrival, Carlton. Prince Henry arrived yesterday and has been telling us all the plans he has for his Kingdom, once he is officially placed on the throne." Carlton knew King Markus to be a very kind and pleasant man, however, he was not one to be toyed with. He was held in high respect by all of those who know him and feared by those who do not.

Carlton bowed, "I am sorry to hear of Queen Lydia's illness, I hope it will not keep us from enjoying her presence while we are here. I am sure that had my mother known she would have come earlier. She and my father will join us later tonight, if that is acceptable to you, Your Majesty?"

"Yes! That would be perfect! Prince Henry has many ideas that I would like your father to hear. Gentlemen, since we will be joined this evening by King Stefen and they are about to begin the Vespers Tourney, I suggest that we adjourn until after the ball tonight." Then looking at Carlton straight in the eyes, he continued, "I know a certain Princess that will never forgive her father if he keeps a certain Prince from dancing with her all night." Slapping Carlton on the back, he left the room.

Everett had a question he'd been stifling, but could now burst free. "Carlton, please tell me about your horses. I have been watching all of the horses that have been brought in for the tournament and I must say that those from your Kingdom seem to be more robust than ours. Is it a different breed?" Prince Everett loved horses, but did not spend as much time in the stables as Carlton had.

Everett and Carlton often spoke of horses and their care. Though they were very close in age, Carlton had been given charge over the mews or stables since he was sixteen. Everett had only a few horses to which he took charge as King Markus still enjoyed having charge of the horses in general.

But, before Carlton could speak, Prince Henry interrupted. "Wait until my horses arrive, Everett. I believe that you will see that Cantwell is not the only Kingdom who can produce a beautiful stallion."

Carlton could see that this was not going to be the enjoyable visit to Breckridge Hall that he had anticipated. It appeared that Prince Henry was determined to outdo him at every turn. *Could it be possible that Henry did not care for him?* No matter, that suited him fine as he was growing a distinct dislike for Henry at a quick pace!

King Stefen and Queen Hannah's arrival was more than welcome. It meant he had at least two confederates and perhaps more importantly, the beginning of the festivities.

The Vespers Tourney was well attended. The royal families of each Kingdom viewed the event from King

Markus' box. There was less pomp than there would be the following day, but everyone enjoyed this tournament. It helped build the excitement for the main event. The first three winners were from Cantwell. This was a great reflection on Carlton and the young men that he had tutored.

Prince Henry was quick to clarify his position, "We did not bring anyone to compete in this event as we believe it is above their station. Ravenswood will only be competing in the jousting event tomorrow."

This comment brought no small stir amongst all of the monarchs. The attitude manifest in Prince Henry was distasteful. Though they were blessed to be of royalty birth, they never presumed to take liberties, they always spoke highly of their people. The monarchs knew that the only way they were able to live as they did was because of the hard work of all of the people in their Kingdom. The peasants, farmers, millers, tinkers, cooks, seamstresses, etc. they all contributed to sustain not only themselves, but those who governed their Kingdom.

King Markus quickly stated his view, "Any ruler knows that if you don't take care of your people all of your Kingdom suffers. We believe that these tournaments are not only for enjoyment and unity, but that those who were born to farmers, for example, who have talents elsewhere, can display it. Many of the most notable knights have been discovered at a Vespers Tourney." King Markus was very kind, but his meaning was clear. Prince Henry was silenced and did not make any other disparaging remarks.

Caroline was seated next to Carlton for the feast. This was one of the first occasions that Carlton attended that he did not have to bribe a housekeeper to switch name cards. To his delight, Prince Henry was on the same side of the table only several seats away. He was seated next to Prince Everett and Countess Marlana, a cousin of Caroline's.

After the main course was served, Carlton, asked, "Would I be lucky enough to enjoy a dance or two with the prettiest woman here? I understand your dances are all taken."

Caroline laughed, "What was I to say? I don't think I like the man."

"So, do you have an opening for me?"

"Don't be silly! I don't have a dance schedule. I was hoping that every dance would be filled like it was in Cantwell?"

"Definitely! I feared you had tired of me already."

Caroline toyed with her food, "How could I tire of the man who not only taught me to ride a horse, but gave me the most beautiful horse I have ever seen?"

"The horse, eh? And I had attributed it to my charming personality!"

"Your Highness, surely you know by now that my head is not turned by just a handsome face or flattery."

As the meal progressed, Carlton kept repeating Caroline's words in his mind. *Just a handsome face or flattery. Exactly what will it take to win this beautiful Princess?*

Carlton had never labored so long to win any prize. However, never was there any such prize placed before him. Whenever he had faced a challenge before, he sought out the master and learned all he could from them. *Who could be his teacher now? Why is it that in matters of such great importance there are no teachers?*

Just as that thought crossed his mind, he looked around the room. Sitting just across the table were their parents. Queen Hannah and Queen Lydia were discussing concerns within their Kingdoms. Each expressing their concerns and receiving advice and council from one another. Their husbands listened in silence. Both Monarchs were genuinely interested in their opinions.

This was the first time he noticed that his father was not only interested in their conversation, but he looked to his wife for his strength as a monarch. Yet, he was the one who made all of the decisions and was the face of the Kingdom. To him came all of the problems and all of the glory. At least that is how Carlton had always seen it.

Now, in their somewhat private conversation, he could see the love and respect in his father's eyes. He needed her. He would not be the ruler or man that he is without her by his side.

Carlton found it hard to take it all in. Suddenly, it seemed he had been given new understanding. He could see and feel things he had never seen or felt before. Looking at King Markus, he saw much of the same. Queen Lydia was his support. *This is what Caroline is looking for. This is what I need to be.* With a smile of realization, Carlton knew that he had the perfect mentors seated in front of him. He must become the perfect student if he wanted to win the heart of the fairest woman he had ever known.

A burst of laughter from Prince Henry turned everyone's attention to him. Seeing that all eyes were on him, he turned toward King Markus and said. "Your Majesty, when will the dance begin? It is getting late and I have secured the promise of a waltz from Princess Caroline. I am first on the field tomorrow and I must get my rest. You see, among other things, I intend to win the competition."

Surprised by his boldness, King Markus looked around the room at his other guests. Seeing that they had no objections, he said, "It appears that Prince Henry is anxious to dance with my daughter. I suggest that we adjourn to the ballroom. As to your winning the contest, you have many contenders. Perhaps Caroline, you should give our guest the first waltz so that he may get the rest he feels he needs."

The look on the King's face, verified to Carlton that King Markus was not impressed with the Prince nor his boldness. Henry obviously had not been taught manners, protocol or decorum.

Caroline's face colored slightly, but she was harder to read. *She just said she didn't like him, but she seems to enjoy the attention from Prince Henry, but why?* He blatantly spoke his mind in front of everyone. He was everything she said she detested. Prideful and flirtatious.

The ball would not be as long as usual. Under very little protest, Prince Henry and Princess Caroline began the ball.

Carlton could not bear to see them together, so he went out to the balcony and watched the festivities that were held for the pages and attendants. He knew that they would be holding their own celebration and thought that it, too, might be a dance.

He did hear music, but it was that of a mandolin. Listening closely he presumed that the minstrel was their entertainment. Recognizing the tune he had played when he told of Prince Henry, Carlton was annoyed. Muttering under his breath he said, "Prince Henry, Prince Henry! I wish I had never heard his name!"

Just then Caroline put her hand on his arm. "Your Highness? I believe the next waltz was to be ours. Are you willing to save a princess in distress? Or do you also have to retire early?"

Grateful and delighted to hear Caroline's voice, Carlton responded appropriately, "My lady, had I known you were in distress, I would have come on my white charger!"

She laughed as they walked on to the dance floor.

After a few dances, Prince Everett interrupted, "My Father has asked for an audience with us in his study. I believe your father is to be there as well. Caroline, Mother suggested that you retire as tomorrow will be a long day."

Once again, Carlton's quest for happiness was interrupted. Caroline nodded her agreement and turned to leave. Carlton held her hand and pulled her back. "Will I see you before the parade tomorrow?"

Smiling, Caroline said, "Of course! I will need to give you my scarf, if you are willing to wear it?"

Moonfaced, Carlton declared, "I would be honored! Thank you."

Everett slapped Carlton on the back and led the way to the study.

"Is there a problem, Everett?"

"I am not sure. Some riders came in from your Kingdom. Father said that King Stefen had been expecting them for several weeks.

As they entered the study, they found both King Markus and King Stefen pacing the floor as they waited for the Princes' arrival.

Carlton was pleased to see that Prince Henry was not in attendance. Carlton and Everett cast each other a questioning glance as King Stefen began to speak.

"Good! Jennings, will you please give us your report again?" asked King Stefen.

Jennings, one of King Stefen's most trusted knights bowed slightly to the King and began to rehearse his adventures of the past several weeks. "As you are now aware, King Stefen asked me to take a small number of men and visit Ravenswood Kingdom. We did not travel in a group, or even as knights. We mingled with the people to learn more about their king and kingdom. We found a very depressed Kingdom, both in resources and attitude. It appears that the farmers are still suffering from a drought that has lasted several years. The people are all near starvation. When asked about their King, their eyes were filled with fear and they would no longer speak with us."

King Markus interrupted, "Did they speak of changing their circumstances – coming to Breckridge Hall or Cantwell?"

"Yes, Your Majesty. Some conversations indicated that if they could, they would leave Ravenswood altogether."

"What is stopping them from leaving?" asked Carlton.

"That is the question we have not been able to have answered, Your Highness. Each of us offered to escort a family or two and they all declined, without explanation. It is my opinion that they are afraid of someone or something."

King Stefen looked directly at King Markus, "We have always maintained that our subjects remain free to travel or move to a different kingdom if they should choose. Maybe King Norman doesn't honor that."

Sir Jennings continued, "Sire, it is hard to describe. It is as if the whole kingdom is suppressed. The land, the animals, the people. I have never seen such a sight in my life! It feels heavy and without hope."

"What could cause such a thing Markus?" asked Stefen.

"I hate to say it, but the only thing I can think of is an oppressive Monarch."

Frustrated, Prince Everett asked, "What about the minstrel? He sings tales of peace, prosperity and joy in Ravenswood!"

Jennings smiled and respectfully replied, "Your Highness, minstrels sing songs they are paid to sing. If you want to promote someone or someplace, you pay a minstrel. My guess is that the minstrel has been well paid."

Prince Everett seemed very disappointed, he muttered under his breath, "The minstrel is dishonest?"

King Stefen had been silent for quite some time. "Thank you Jennings! Well done! Please keep the findings and our discussion to yourself. Instruct your men to do the same. Please enjoy the festivities. We will talk again after the tournament is over."

Jennings bowed to both Monarchs and left the room.

"Father, what do you think?" asked Carlton.

"I am not sure what is going on, I suggest that we keep a careful eye on Prince Henry and anyone from his Kingdom. The pieces to this puzzle are coming together, albeit quite slowly. Let's keep a close watch, but silently- we don't want to cause concern. We also don't want to put them on guard. We want to see the *real* Prince Henry."

"What about the Princess? Surely we should make her aware of it so that she won't continue to associate with him?" Carlton sounded concerned and hopeful.

With an understanding smile, the King kindly responded, "No son, we won't tell the Princess or any of the women yet. The more people that know, the harder it will be to unravel this mystery. Remember to keep your eyes and ears alert."

"I suggest we get a good night's sleep. I am matched up against Prince Henry for the tournament," Everett stated with obvious annoyance.

It was indeed a long night for everyone. Prince Carlton did not sleep well. He was not worried about the tournament, it was Caroline. Carlton had never been so nervous before a tournament. However, never before was there so much at stake! Breakfast was brought to him in his room. He would not see anyone until the parading of colors.

The parading of colors and crests had been a bit bewildering to Carlton. He had fully expected to be wearing Caroline's scarf as a token of her support. However, he had not seen Princess Caroline since their dance the night before. *Could Prince Henry of Ravenswood have turned her head? No, Henry was not wearing a pink scarf, but neither am I.* Carlton was seething inside, what happened?

Now it was time for the competition and Caroline was still nowhere to be seen. Her chair in the observation tower remained empty as it had during the first two matches. Only one more match and it was Carlton's turn. He was to compete against Lord Kirkham of Breckridge.

King Markus had changed the final match. Prince Henry was originally to be first on the field, however, since he had drawn Prince Everett as an opponent, their match was to be the final one.

Just as Carlton mounted his horse, Princess Caroline appeared, she was completely out of breath, and noticeably upset. "I am sorry I am late! I had an emergency. Please, will you still wear my scarf?"

"Of course, Your Highness, It will be an honor! Is everything alright?" Carlton leaned over the side of the horse with his right arm extended. Princess Caroline tied her pale pink scarf on his arm just above his elbow.

Before she could respond and before he could kiss her hand, the Master of Ceremonies called for Prince Carlton of Cantwell and Lord Kirkham of Breckridge Hall. Caroline smiled and hurried to the observation box.

Where had she been? She said it was an emergency, but everyone else seemed to be in their places. Everyone except for Prince Henry. Had she been with him? Carlton knew he must focus on the competition ahead of him. He would not represent Cantwell or the Princess if he let his mind dwell on her absence. So far, there had been no real challenger. Each of the previous contenders had earned a point or two, but nothing that Carlton considered a real challenge. Everett was a great horseman and he knew that he would have to work hard to best him. As for Prince Henry, Carlton did not know what kind of a contest to expect.

Carlton, sat facing his opponent. His horse was steady and as anxious to perform as he was. Lord Kirkham was wearing a green colored scarf. No doubt a gift, such as Carlton's. They rode to the center of the field with their face guard in place. Showing little than their eyes. They gave each other a nod of the head and went back to their side to prepare for the match. Carlton's page stood holding his first lance. After closing his helmet, Carlton took the lance. He was ready for their first set. The horn blew and both riders were off, lances extended and prepared to strike their opponent.

Prince Carlton was first to strike, breaking the tip of the lance as he hit Lord Kirkham's shield. Lord Kirkham, startled by the strike dropped his lance and the first run score was three to zero. Both riders returned to their page to receive their second lance. Carlton was off to a good start.

The first lance gave each knight a chance to see how their opponent would respond, so the second run was easier to calculate. Prince Carlton knew that his challenger was not skilled at jousting. No doubt he had been convinced to compete by the beautiful girl who bestowed her scarf upon him. Even though Carlton felt that he understood his opponent, he still could not let down his guard. He had to best him, not just for Caroline but he was competing against Prince Everett and Prince Henry. The winner would be chosen by the highest score from each set of riders.

The second run was much like the first. Prince Carlton's lance tip shattered as it met with Lord Kirkham's breast plate. Of course he was protected by his armor, however, the impact nearly knocked him off of his horse. The score for round two was four to zero. With a total score of seven to zero, Prince Carlton was now tied with Lord DeVry of Ravenswood Kingdom.

The third run found Lord Kirkham sitting on the paddock! He was so busy looking into the stands, that he did not brace himself for the impact of Carlton's lance. Other than bruised pride, he would recover quickly. Before the score could be announced he was limping off the paddock with his arm around a pretty little maiden in a green dress. Even though the score announced for the third set was 5 to 0, making Carlton's total score 13, Lord Kirkham had won the prize he had competed for.

Prince Everett and Prince Henry had already met in the middle and acknowledged each other before Carlton had a chance to dismount his horse. Carlton watched the contest from the contestant pavilion. Everett did not brandish a scarf but Carlton saw many a maiden both noble and peasant wishing that he was wearing her scarf. Prince Everett was quite comely or so that is what his mother called it.

The first run was quick and both men broke the tip of their lances. The judges called it 3 to 3. Neither man was dislodged. They seemed to be equally matched.

On the second run, Everett's lance shattered upon contact with Prince Henry's shield and the tip of Henry's lance broke. The score for this run was 4 to 2 in Everett's favor, making their total scores 7 to 5 in Prince Everett's favor.

The third and final run had the attention of all of the audience. Not even a baby dared to cry or coo. As they waited for the trumpet to signal the start, Carlton thought he saw the sun catch a glare on Prince Henry's lance. *Was that a blade? Impossible! That was forbidden. Surely, I am mistaken.* Carlton had no time to stop the match. As Henry and Everett met, Prince Henry's horse stumbled and his lance sank deep into Everett's left thigh.

The crowd gasped. Carlton ran onto the paddock along with Thorndyke, Jennings and several pages and servants. Carlton caught Everett as he began to fall off of his horse. Prince Henry looked upset, but not as much as Carlton thought he should, had it truly been an accident.

A group of men carried Prince Everett into the Castle after the lance had been removed and a tourniquet applied to his leg. King Markus calmly dismissed the people before he left the competition.

Queen Lydia, Hannah and Caroline followed closely as Prince Everett was taken to his room.

A few knights escorted Prince Henry to the King's study. King Stefen and Prince Carlton also went to the study neither of them spoke until they arrived.

King Markus invited them in and then calmly but sternly said, "Prince Henry, explain yourself. If you can."

"Your Majesty, I beg your forgiveness. My horse stumbled. I never would have struck his leg. I am well aware that the rules state above the waist."

"Why did you have a blade on your spear?" demanded Carlton. Carlton knew that it was not his place to question the Prince, but he did not know if King Markus was aware that his lance had a blade.

Ignoring Prince Carlton, Henry looked directly at King Markus and said, "I am new to your customs. In Ravenswood on the third run, the knights are always equipped with a blade. It makes the third run more competitive. Perhaps I should have acquainted myself with your traditions. Had my horse not tripped, Prince Everett's shield or breast plate would have been ample protection. I do hope that Prince Everett will be heal quickly."

Prince Henry then stood and asked if he could be excused. "It has been a long day for all of us and I am sure you will want to see to Prince Everett. Please give him my apologies." He left the room without being dismissed or any further conversation.

Carlton waited until the prince had left before he addressed the King. "Your Majesty, I don't believe his horse stumbled. I was watching from the tents and Prince Henry made his horse stumble."

"Now son, I know you don't like the Prince, but I don't believe he would fake a stumble just to strike my son."

"I do." King Stefen spoke quietly, however his words were filled with emotion. "I saw it too Markus! When Henry was within three feet of Everett, he pulled left on the reigns just enough to make his horse back up then he immediately pulled right urging him forward. I know I haven't ridden a lot since the accident, but I still know horses. I began to doubt what I had seen until Carlton confirmed it. Let's speak with Everett after he is well enough. I believe he may have seen it also!"

"Well then, what do we do with the tournament? Everyone is waiting for the outcome."

"Prince Henry should be disqualified if for no other reason than the blade," stated Stefen.

"He claims that a blade is acceptable on the third run as far as his Kingdom is concerned. He felt no remorse on that account," King Markus was perplexed.

"That form of jousting has not been practiced for many years. In fact, Prince Henry was not born when blades were used in jousting. I don't believe we were born when that rule existed! Where was he educated?" Carlton had never seen his father so enraged. " At the very least, he must be disqualified! If you overlook the use of the blade and the injury to the leg, you are not only doing Everett a disservice, but opening the door for others to use a friendly competition as a way to settle a score or an onset for war. You must think of the Kingdom, Markus," King Stefen urged. In the back of Stefen's mind he recalled the threats Cantwell had received from King Norman, Henry's Grandfather. *But why Everett? What did he have against King Markus and Breckridge Hall?*

"I am sure that you are right. Stefen."

"Let's check on Everett before we address the crowd."

"Father, do you think that Henry is trying to begin a war between our Kingdoms?" asked Carlton thoughtfully.

"I don't know son, either he is a foolish young man, or he has come to do just that. We must keep on alert without letting the people see our concern. We don't want to aid him in his campaign, whatever it may be."

Everett was resting, and the physician had been able to stop the bleeding. "He has lost a lot of blood Your Majesty he is weak but he will recover."

"Yes, I will not think otherwise. Is everything cleaned up so that the women can come in? His mother will not rest until she sees him."

"Yes sire, but he should be allowed to rest as much as possible. A short visit would be best."

"Thank you, Manning. I will place a guard in the room and one just outside the door."

"Of course Sire, I will stay close and send for you should there be any change."

"Yes, see that you do."

The door opened and Queen Lydia and Queen Hannah rushed inside. Princess Caroline was not far behind them. Lydia had obviously been crying.

"Manning says he will recover. He has lost a lot of blood, so he is weak. We will place guards inside the room and just outside. Manning, the Physician, will alert us of any changes."

"Could it have been intentional? Would Prince Henry try to kill him?" Queen Lydia was rightfully concerned.

"No dear, he said it was an accident, that his horse stumbled. I am posting the guards to alert us of his recovery that is all."

"Why the blade father? The lances are supposed to be out of wood and dull, no sharp tips!" Caroline was as frustrated as Carlton had been.

"Prince Henry tells us that in his Kingdom, the blade is always used on the third run. They don't usually have injuries because of the protection of the shield and armor. They do respect the rule of above the waist. It was just an accident."

This information seemed to satisfy the women.

"We are going to dismiss the lingering crowd. We don't want to have the people speculating and worrying about Everett. Remember, just stay a few more minutes, and then let him rest." King Markus kissed Lydia on the cheek and the Monarchs left to quiet the crowd. After he had assured the people that Prince Everett was well and resting, King Markus announced the disqualification of Prince Henry due to the unauthorized use of the blade tipped lance. With Prince Henry's elimination, Carlton had won the match. Under the circumstances it wasn't fitting to continue the celebration. The King thanked the people for coming and concluded the festivity. A somber crowd exited the competition field.

Carlton watched as the small company from Ravenswood left the castle grounds to begin their journey home. Prince Henry was nowhere to be seen. After a few minutes, he saw Henry riding his horse toward the gates. In his hand he held a bouquet of pink flowers tied with a pink scarf! *Surely Caroline would not give him her scarf after all that had happened?* Then he saw her, Princess Caroline was walking slowly toward the stables. It appeared that she had indeed given her scarf to Prince Henry.

Prince Henry left the grounds with a bouquet wrapped in a pink ribbon. Carlton was frustrated with the whole affair. If only he could speak with his mother. Queen Hannah was the only person he knew that could understand women. He would seek her counsel as soon as Prince Everett was on the mend. He wanted to go home, to Cantwell, he would not force himself upon a woman that had eyes for another. However, he knew that leaving before Prince Everett recovered would be an insult to Breckridge Hall. When he was sure that the Princess had left the stables, he would go for a ride. Riding was another way that Prince Carlton was able to clear his mind of female distractions.

As Carlton prepared for his ride, a servant boy knocked on his door. "King Markus and King Stefen request your presence in the study. Please make haste!"

Carlton abandoned his riding gloves and hurried to the study. There he found both of the monarchs pacing anxiously waiting for his arrival. "What's wrong, Sire? Has Prince Everett taken a turn for the worse?"

King Markus' furrowed brow softened a little. "No Carlton, we have received news of Ravenswood and require your assistance."

"Of course! What can I do?"

"A courier just arrived with news of imprisonments, torture and possible war. If your father or I leave right now, it will cause great alarm to both Kingdoms. Prince Carlton, will you go with a selection of knights and learn what you can? It is hard to believe that King Norman is capable of such things."

"Immediately, Your Majesty!"

"Son, this is not a mere expedition. It must be handled with a cool head and diplomacy. We are not trying to start a war. Our hope is that you can travel incognito and gather accurate information. Then return and let us know what you find. Should you find the reports to be true, send word post haste! Do not proceed until we have arrived with our armies to support you. Do you understand?"

"Yes Father, I will leave within the hour."

"Take care son, we, none of us, have had much to do with Ravenswood for over a decades. We don't know what you might encounter. Remember to keep a cool head and use diplomacy. This is a time to set aside personal feelings. I don't know where you are emotionally, but we must protect our people. Our kingdoms need you."

"I understand Father, what will you tell Mother and Caroline?"

"Just that we had sent you on an errand that could not wait. They will understand. You may tell Caroline good-bye if you wish, but remember, you are not to speak of your errand or of our suspicions."

"Yes, Father. I will leave her a parchment, I believe it will be the best way."

Leaving a parchment was definitely the best way. *How can I face her now? Especially when I am going to spy on the man whom she cares for.* Oh how it pained Carlton to even think of it! *I have finally found my true love and know the joy of loving and being in love. Then in only a few days, her head is turned to another. Have I been too hasty? Was she really so fickle?*

As Carlton began to write her a parchment, he felt a surge of chivalry. *I will not give her up without a battle.* Carlton took the ink well and penned a letter that he had wanted to write for several weeks now. He confessed his undying love for her and his desire to spend the rest of their lives together. He spoke of her beauty not just physical, but her inner beauty. Then, knowing how much she loved flowers, he instructed her lady-in-waiting, Clara, to pick some pink flowers and deliver it to her along with the parchment. However, she should wait until after Carlton had left to deliver it.

Princess Caroline was still in the stables when the flowers arrived. The bouquet was a few pink carnations and several chrysanthemums and a cyclamen.

Caroline sat heart broken, "Who sent this Clara?"

"His Highness, Prince Carlton, miss."

"Is he gone?"

"Yes, Miss. He rode off 'bout an hour ago."

"And he asked you to bring me *these* flowers?"

"Yes, Your Highness. What's wrong with them? Are they not your favorite color? He said to choose pink."

She was heartbroken, because of what the flowers said: You're a wonderful friend, resignation, I'll never forget you, Good-bye. Caroline tossed the flowers aside and went into the stable with Ginger. "Well, Ginger, you have to get well now. You and Carlton were to be my future, now he has left me. Don't you leave me too?" Caroline began to cry.

If only I had been able to see Carlton before the competition. But I had to see to Ginger! Someone had given her horse nightshade. Caroline found a few petals laced in with her hay. *Oh, how I wish I could talk to Carlton. He would know what to do. He was acting strangely though, he seemed reluctant to wear my scarf at the tournament. When I saw him in Everett's room, he would not acknowledge me. Not even with a smile. What have I done? What am I to do? When can I see him alone and get my questions answered?*

Everett was good with horses, but he would not be available to consult with for a few days. Would it be too late? Desperate, Caroline was going to talk with the stable boy when Prince Henry came to get his horse.

Henry saw the state she was in and asked, "Princess Caroline, you seem distraught. May I assist you?"

Surprised to see him, Caroline was caught off-guard. She was so concerned about Ginger. She had heard that Henry was familiar with horses, probably more of a horseman than Everett. Caroline reluctantly explained her dilemma to the Prince. He graciously offered to look at the horse and give whatever assistance was within his power.

"Do you know how much nightshade the horse has digested?"

"No I don't. I found a few petals mixed in with her hay. I don't know if she ate any. I know that the leaves and stems would be more dangerous even fatal to her. I discarded everything in her manger and had it cleaned before giving her fresh hay."

"Impressive! I am surprised that a woman of your station would be so familiar with the plant and its uses."

"I know some, I have a great love of horses. How will I know if she actually ate some? What can I do?"

"Look for these symptoms, dry mouth, change in heart rate, muscle tremors, laying down excessively. If you notice any of these, send for me immediately! Otherwise, all you can do is keep a close eye on her. She is lucky to have such an attentive master."

"Your Highness, how do you think this may have happened?"

"You say it was in her manger? Where do they get her feed? Someone unfamiliar with nightshade must have mixed it with her feed. I am sure no one would knowingly poison her. Perhaps when they exercised her this morning. If she digested a great deal of nightshade you will know within the next few hours. Otherwise, if you caught it in time, she may just need a few days' rest. I wouldn't suggest riding her again today. However, a gentle walk would do her good."

"Thank you, Prince Henry! You have been most helpful. How can I ever repay you?"

"No need, Princess. Wait, there is a way." Looking at the Princess, he saw a bouquet of pink ambrosia sitting on a stool in the stable, wrapped in one of her pink ribbons. It was meant to be for Carlton after he was officially named the winner of the tournament. "I would love to take a beautiful pink ribbon back with me to remind me of your beauty!"

Grateful for his help and knowing that Prince Henry did not understand their meaning, not as Carlton did. She hesitantly gave him the bouquet with her sincere gratitude. She watched as he left the mews.

All she could do now was wait and watch. Silently she prayed for her beautiful horse. A gift from the only man she would ever truly love.

I cannot believe that Carlton would leave in such a way. Caroline sat looking at the discarded flowers. *If only Carlton had cared enough to talk to me before he left. Not even a parchment.* She was startled when she heard a man behind her clear his throat. "Begging your pardon, my lady, His Highness Prince Henry requests permission to enter."

Wiping her eyes and trying very hard to collect herself, she nodded and Prince Henry entered.

"Your Highness, it seems I have come at a most inopportune time."

"No, please, come in. Have you forgotten something?"

"Yes, Your Highness. I had not traveled far, when I realized that I could not return to my Kingdom without at least a hope that I would be able to see you again."

"What?"

"Surely you have sensed my adoration in the few days that I have been here? Please tell me that I may have a chance to win your heart."

Caroline found herself at a complete loss of words. Prince Henry, interested in her?

"Would you consider coming to my Kingdom to meet my grandfather? I know it is typically improper, however, he is celebrating his 90th birthday in a few days' time and he is quite unwell. I know it would bring him great pleasure to meet such a beautiful Princess. It would also give us opportunity to get to know one another."

Sensing her hesitation, he added, "I will take your mare, Ginger with me and see to her healing personally. When you come, she will be there and well."

If Caroline had any misgivings at first, Prince Henry's closing statements made her forget them. Here was the answer to her biggest problem. Of course her heart was hurting because of Prince Carlton's rejection, but she had to put that aside now. She must focus on healing Ginger and Prince Henry was her only option.

Seeing that she had justified it in her mind, Henry continued. "Good! I will take her with me now and see to her every comfort. Promise me that you will leave tomorrow. I will send my best carriage to meet you at the Lazy Horse Inn. It lies just outside of Cantwell, a two days journey. I shall arrange for your stay and I will have my most comfortable carriage take you from the Inn to Ravenswood. It is only a three days journey from there."

Henry motioned for his valet to bridle Ginger and prepare her for travel.

"Will travelling that distance be too difficult for Ginger?"

With only a slight hesitation, Henry said, "You discovered the night shade a few hours ago, correct?"

"Yes, Your Highness."

"I believe that you caught it just in time. If she had eaten too much of it, she would have reacted differently. Walking will help her get through this. I will see that she does not run and that no one rides her until you arrive in Ravenswood."

Turning to his servant, he ordered, "Don't bother bringing a saddle, put on her blanket and bridle only."

Ginger seemed very agitated as the servant bridled her. "I am sorry, Ginger is usually very friendly around strangers," Caroline apologized.

"She is not quite herself now, but when you see her in Ravenswood in one weeks' time, your mare will be feeling better!" Prince Henry gave Caroline a slight bow, kissed her gloved hand and mounted his horse. "Come James! Let's go while there is still light."

Caroline watched as Prince Henry led Ginger out of the stables and through the palace gates. It all happened so quickly. Did she do the right thing? Had it not been for Ginger's illness, Caroline knew she would never have agreed to visit Ravenswood. Prince Henry had caught her in a weak moment. She made a decision without taking time to think it through.

Henry's appearance was timely, Ginger would receive the attention she needed and possibly save her life. Not only that, but Caroline could possibly have a second chance at love.

No, she knew that she would never love anyone the way she loved Prince Carlton! Perhaps in time she could learn to care for Prince Henry. She could not believe her thoughts – were they really her thoughts? How could she dismiss her feelings for Prince Carlton so quickly? How could he have left without even leaving her a note?

Leaving the stable she went to check on Everett. She found her mother and Queen Hannah in quiet, but deep conversation. She did not want to disturb them. Everett was resting and the physician had left for the day. This was all Caroline needed to know, her brother and the heir to the throne of Breckridge Hall was on the mend.

When she inquired after her father, she was told that he and King Stefen were in conference and had given instructions not to be disturbed.

Caroline retired to her quarters and sent for her lady in waiting, Clara. She told her of their travel plans and instructed her to make all the preparations, without telling the servants. She would leave a note to be delivered to her mother telling her of her visit to Ravenswood Kingdom, with instructions that they be given to her a day following her departure.

She knew that with her brother's accident and the recent celebrations, the Queens would take their tea in Everett's room and the Monarchs would most likely eat in the study. She would be well on her way to Ravenswood before they learned of her plans.

Perhaps in some small way, she could mend the relationship with the Kingdoms. That in itself would be a benefit to all. For some reason, Carlton had distanced himself from her. Prince Henry would help care for Ginger, and Caroline would be back before they even really missed her. It would only be a fortnight and everything would be back to normal.

Part 11

Caroline let the door close quietly behind her. She didn't look back, she didn't dare. *What is there for me anyway?* She thought she had poured her heart out to Carlton. *Hadn't I asked him to wear my scarf? He seemed to enjoy my company. Why, he even gave me Ginger! What had I done to make him change his mind? He hadn't even shown enough courtesy to respond to my expression of admiration. What a fool I had been – he hadn't really changed, stupid minstrels, I let them bias my thoughts! I really wanted him to love me ... that was it.*

She was working hard to convince herself that there was no feeling in her heart for Prince Carlton. *What did it matter anyway? I have to let it go – it was past. I will look forward, on to a new journey, a new adventure, as father would say.*

She used a small linen handkerchief to dab her eyes dry and vowed she would never entertain thoughts of Prince Carlton again. She was on her way to Ravenswood, to Prince Henry. She knew little about him, he too had been courting her of sorts. While he was there in Breckridge Hall he was very attentive to her. He was very attractive, more so than Carlton, but her heart had been drawn to Carlton.

There he was again. *Go away!* She could no longer direct her thoughts from Prince Carlton and she began to sob. Her lady in waiting would not share any of these events with anyone—it would be as though it had never happened. It was better to let it out now, before they arrived at the Inn or Ravenswood Castle *–what kind of name is that? It sounds depressing and dark.* Caroline shook her head as though it would loosen the heart wrenching thoughts from her. What did it matter? This emotional release would be good for her heart and her mind.

It took two days to reach the Lazy Horse Inn. They arrived just after nightfall. Here, her coach and driver would leave her. She and Clara, would spend the night and in the morning Prince Henry's carriage would arrive to take them to their final destination, Ravenswood Kingdom. Because it was so close to Cantwell, Caroline's thoughts lingered just a bit. Oh how she wished she could spend a few hours in Queen Hannah's gardens. They always seemed to bring her peace. *Why would Carlton leave so suddenly? Why didn't he at least say good bye in person? Only a bunch of flowers that said "we can only be friends."*

Sleep did not come as easily as Caroline had hoped. She wished, as she had never wished before, that she was resting peacefully in her home and native kingdom. Never had she made such an important decision in such a short time.

She knew that she was acting out of anger and hurt. She loved Prince Carlton so much and he had no room in his heart for her. She realized that no distance would ease her pain. She would simply tell the coach driver to take her back home.

Then she remembered Ginger, she knew she had to press on. Knowing that Prince Henry would soon be King, he had sought her out as a potential partner, a wife. Since Caroline had no other offers, she feared that she would eventually marry as part of an alliance with another Kingdom. After all, is that not what her mother had done?

Lydia and King Stefen were engaged to be married. It was only the night before the wedding that they each chose to marry a stranger for the benefit of their Kingdom. *They were deeply in love. Mine is an unrequited love. They would expect, and I should do the same.*

The following day, three carriages arrived just after the morning meal. Two were plain coaches, black with a gold trim. The third carriage was the one that caught her eye. Never had Caroline seen such a beautiful, ornate coach. There were carvings of cherubim's and roses inlaid with, what appeared to be, real gold.

The coachman seemed amiable and was very kind to Caroline. He did however seem to be on a tight schedule and insisted that they leave right away. "Begging your pardon, Your Highness, we must be on our way. Thompson will meet us at the turn off. If we are not there promptly, it will be my job!"

"Who is Thompson?"

"The Steward's wife. She is the only one that he would trust with such a charge. I dare not anger her miss." He quickly placed Caroline's bags on one of the black coaches.

Caroline and Clara followed his lead and went to the golden carriage. The inside was just as beautiful as the outside and Caroline found herself smiling with pleasure. *Perhaps this can be a pleasant adventure after all!*

Princess Caroline had never been one to have her head turned by jewels and gold. Their Kingdom, had never taxed their people in excess. Her father did not believe in glutting himself on the labors of the people he served. This was her first real glimpse of Ravenswood. Perhaps it is a Kingdom which abounds in wealth? She was determined not to judge the King nor his grandson prematurely. *This may just be his way of welcoming me to their Kingdom.*

Caroline was beginning to feel more settled, until the carriage came to an abrupt stop.

Clara looked out the window in fear, "Surely we have not been met by Highwaymen!"

Whispering, Caroline asked, "What do you see, Clara?"

"Two riders on horseback. A man and a woman. It appears they mean to join us Your Highness."

Soon an elderly woman, neatly dressed completely in black stepped up into the carriage. "Your Highness, Prince Henry sends his regards. I am Thompson the housekeeper.

I will see you safely to the castle and help you get settled in."

"Thank you, Thompson, how thoughtful of you"

"Mr. Thompson, the Kings Steward, will ride with the driver."

The ride in the coach was long and boring. Clara had been able to sleep, but sleep would not come to Caroline. She longed to be heading for another place. As she pondered her miserable state, she looked out across the hillside. Dusk was falling, perhaps there would be a sunset that might lift her spirits.

She stared into the dimly lit forest. No. It was not a forest. A forest has trees, lots of trees. The best she could call this was the ugly remains of what once could have been a beautiful forest. There were stumps of trees that had been first ravaged for its timber, but it looked as though a devastating fire had hurried through a very dry forest – there were no leaves or needles on any trees and the ground had absolutely no foliage whatsoever.

She became alarmed and uneasy, in her heart she knew that something was very wrong. But, she did not know what. She decided to take a chance and express her concerns. As she looked around the coach, she noticed that Thompson was watching her. Her stare was fixed and strong.

Caroline wondered if Thompson was aware of the change in atmosphere, would she be able to feel the new distress that Caroline was feeling? That is when it occurred to Caroline that Thompson was not here to protect her, but rather to insure her arrival to Ravenswood. She was there to see that Caroline did not turn back.

Courage and determination slowly replaced fear and confusion. Caroline felt that she was not just heading toward danger, but that she was already captive in a world she knew nothing about. One thing she did know, she must not show fear. *Fear can and will consume you if you let it. If Clara and I are going to escape this nightmare, I will have to use my head.*

As a princess, she had been taught to hide her feeling and to never react. She had practiced this somewhat, but never would her acting need to be as convincing as it did now. She must rely on her talents to see her through this. As she mentally reviewed her situation, she knew that Clara would be of little or no help to her. Clara was an innocent, kind and helpful servant. However, she did not think things through. She scared easily, was forgetful and had to be told every move to make. That was partially why Caroline liked her, Caroline could ask her to do things that were not quite proper and Clara had no qualms following her directions. It was because Clara was her lady in waiting, Caroline had been able to go to the stables and cook in the kitchens.

Knowing that the castle was still a day or so away, Princess Caroline decided to take a chance. She would leave a message of warning behind if she could. As the carriage drove on, she began to see that the stumps in the trees were moving. They appeared to be interested and scared at the same time.

If Clara were awake, she would probably be afraid that they were highwaymen. A highwayman right now, it seemed, would be a blessing. Casually reaching for her bag, she found some parchment and a quill. Thompson appeared to be resting and Caroline was careful not to disturb her. She quickly scribbled a note, as encoded as possible. In the note she asked that her parents send seeds of lavender and monkshead. She closed it by stating that they would remind her of home and she would love to get them as soon as possible.

Although Caroline had never seen an enchanted forest, she had heard of their existence. It was her hope that one of these stumps, if that was indeed what they were, would see her note safely to Cantwell. She knew that if Cantwell received a message such as this they would send it by courier immediately to Breckridge Hall, to her mother and Queen Hannah.

When she asked Thompson to stop the coach, she resisted, "We will be at a cottage soon, 'Milady."

Acknowledging her reply, Caroline said, "Please ask the driver to stop, I need to stretch my legs." Caroline was polite, but firm.

Realizing that Caroline would not be dissuaded, Thompson ordered the carriage to stop.

"We mustn't go far from the coach Your Highness, 'tis not safe here."

"You needn't accompany me, Thompson. Clara will be grateful for the opportunity to stand as well." Clara, who had wakened by the sudden stop of the coach was willing but still filled with sleep.

Regardless of her assurance Caroline was to be accompanied by Mr. Thompson.

Caroline knew she must not let her fear show in her voice or expressions. She tried to casually step down from the carriage, knowing that her safety as well as that of Clara would depend on how well she could play the part of a tired, but content Princess.

In her hand she held the note she had penned earlier in the day. She must find a rock or a stone to place it under. It would be hard to do so without being noticed by Thompson who hadn't released her gaze, or Mr. Thompson who was following her along as the *stretched her legs.*

Having had no opportunity to be completely alone, Caroline waited while Clara climbed back inside. She was careful to let the parchment drop just as she climbed back into the coach. Hopefully the wind would carry it to a trustworthy man who would see that her father received it. Although it was addressed to the King, she knew her mother would understand her coded message.

They spent the night in what appeared to be one of the Kings hunting lodges. Every possible convenience was there and there were more servants in attendance than Cantwell or Breckridge Hall ever retained for such a party. Other than Caroline's growing unease, she had a comfortable night. As she awoke in the morning, the silence engulfed her. That was it! It was the lack of birds singing and squirrels chatter. Why, even the bees were silenced. It was an eerie silence. This is what brought on her unease, more so than the dead forest.

The day continued in ominous silence. The trees and shrubs became scarce. Caroline sat in sorrow. How could one live with no flowers or greenery? Each turn of the carriage took her further from home and from all of the natural beauties of the earth and from the man she truly loved.

She looked out of the carriage and saw only miles and miles of rock. She tried to find some beauty in it, but she desperately missed her home.

Part 12

Carlton rode at the head of his men. He had never before seen a landscape such as this. Sentinels stood hundreds of feet high. There appeared to be soldiers that were guarding a secret. He was glad to leave this place.

He and his men had been in the Ravenswood Kingdom for two weeks now. It was time to report their finding to the monarchs and take the next step. Never had Prince Carlton seen such blatant abuse of power and birth.

This was another moment that Carlton was grateful for his father. Carlton knew that he himself was not prepared to make such a decision as was laid before his Kingdom now. He took comfort in the fact that the people of Ravenswood were displeased with their King, but concerned because they were preparing for an uprising. Should his father decided to join them, it would not surprise Carlton.

They approached the Lazy Horse Inn and went immediately to the stables. Travelling incognito Carlton joined his men in unsaddling his horse and seeing to his own needs. The stable boys quickly came with candles to offset the oncoming dust and aide in their duties. After a quick curry Carlton turned toward the Inn. But his eye was caught by one horse in particular. There in the stable he saw Ginger! *No, it couldn't be.*

"Boy! Where did you get that horse?" Carlton's request startled the boy, but soon he relaxed and related his tale.

"Oh, that one. A beauty ain't she? I came by her quite skillfully!"

"Pray tell!" Carlton exhibited every bit of patience he could with the lad.

"'Bout three weeks ago, Prince Henry comes through ya sees, and he asks if I has anything that can make a horse sick or even dead. I tells him that nightshade will do it every time. So, he tells me to fetch him some. I comes back with just a wee bit and asks him who it is for. He tells me that there is a Princess who loves a horse and if he could heal the thing he could win her heart. So, I gives him just a wee bit.

"Then he comes back after the tournament and brings this beautiful mare with him. He says that the nightshade worked out fine! He said that he doesn't think that the mare ate any of it and I am to care for it real good until he comes again. He says I can ride it and everything. He says that I maybe can keep it."

Handing him a coin, Prince Carlton asked, "Has the mare been sick at all? Did she indeed get the nightshade?"

"No, sir." Looking at the coin Carlton had placed in his palm and hoping to get another, he said, "I knows another tale of Prince Henry, would you like to hear it?"

Carlton nodded to the boy.

"He not only got her horse, but she herself was here two weeks ago. Going to the King's 90th birthday so she thinks. Me thinks that she is headed for her new home."

"What makes you say that lad? Is she smitten with him?"

"No," he said laughing. "She is pining after that Prince Carlton. Me mum heard her crying in the night. Sayin how the Prince up and left her with nothin but a bouquet of flowers that said, he only wants to be her friend. Mum says that is why she agreed to go to Ravenswood. Her heart is broke."

"Why do you say it is her new home?"

The boy looked sheepishly at his now empty palm and then up at Carlton.

Shaking his head, Carlton placed another coin in his hand. Then holding two more above it he asked again, "What makes you think it will be her new home?"

"'Cause nobody ever comes back from Ravenswood, lest they be in a box."

Carlton placed the coins in the lads palm and joined his men in the Inn. After a quick meal they met in the stables again.

When they were saddled Carlton took his valet with him and decided to send the others back to Breckridge Hall with their report. A peasant woman and the boy interrupted them just before they reached the road.

Her son pointed Carlton out and then the woman addressed him, "Sir, may I speak with ye?"

Carlton nodded, thinking that she was looking for a few more coins he said, "I'll give you a coin if you have useful information."

The woman's face reddened, "I am not looking for coins, sir. Are you at all acquainted with the Princess Caroline?"

"Perhaps, why?"

"A week ago a man came to the inn with a note from her." The woman then handed Carlton a paper.

"We think it might be 'portant, but neither of us can read. She's a dear, that one. Will ye sees that it gets to the King?"

"Yes mam, I shall see to it." Carlton reached into his vest pocket to fetch some coins but the woman and her son were gone.

Carlton quickly read the note. It did sound cryptic, but asked for assistance. He sent the note with the guards going to Breckridge Hall. Before he could turn his horse toward Ravenswood, the woman came running out of the inn hailing him once again. She was distraught. Carlton dismounted and faced the woman. With tears in her eyes she recognized Carlton for who he was and began to bow. Carlton held her up, and with a warning look, begged her to remain standing.

"What is the problem Ma'am?"

Although unable to read, the inn keeper was not dumb! Whispering she said, "Bless you, Your Highness! A man is in the stable to take the Princess' horse. He is sure to take her to Ravenswood or to dispose of the poor thing. My son cannot tell which it is. Either way, I believe the man is up to no good!"

"We will see to it ma'am." Nodding his head he whispered, "Keep my secret my lady, it just may save the Princess's life."

They hurried to the stables where they found the young lad and a middle aged man at odds with each other. "May we be of assistance?" Carlton offered the boy.

Relief washed over his face as the young lad rushed to Carlton's side. "This man says he has Prince Henry's permission to dispose of the mare. Prince Henry told me to hold it until he himself came for her. He said she belonged to Princess Caroline."

Addressing the rider, Carlton asked, "What say ye? Where is the Prince?"

Seeing that he was not going to be able to do as he desired, the man asked to speak privately with Carlton.

Keeping in clear view of his valet and the boy, but definitely out of hearing distance, Carlton awaited his explanation.

"You see, the Prince wants me to bring the horse back so that the fair Princess will like him and consider him for marriage. T'would be the worst thing she could do. Such a lovely lass and consigned to such a prison."

"So, why kill the horse?"

"If the horse lives, she will feel obligated to marry the Prince. He concocted the whole thing, purchased night shade, put it in the manger, and came to help her when she thought no one else could. Can't you see? She would feel an obligation to stay with him."

"You distrust the Prince? Yet you, yourself are trusted enough to fulfill his errand?"

"He has my family hostage. If I don't return, they will be severely punished."

"How many men did you bring with you?" asked Carlton.

"Only two, it would not take more than three of us to pick up the horse." The servant could tell that Carlton was up to something.

"We have visited parts of your Kingdom these past few days. It appears that some are loyal to their Kingdom and some are not. Which are you?" Carlton did not have time to speak in riddles, he had to know with whom he was speaking. This man was concerned about Princess Caroline, so he must not be completely loyal to the King.

"Sir, had you spent more time in our Kingdom, you would have found that there are no loyal subjects, only prisoners. I am Prince Henry's Valet. I have only been at the castle now since his return from school. I left with the prince 20 years ago, when he was just a boy. The kingdom I left is nothing like the one that exists now."

Carlton decided to trust this man, at least a little. "We are from Cantwell, we have been sent by King Stefen and King Markus to bring Princess Caroline home. We have seen your Kingdom from afar. With the lack of foliage, we have not been able to approach the Castle. Will you allow us accompany you to the castle in the place of your two men?"

Although the man had not yet responded, Carlton felt relief. He had been trying to find a way to enter into the Kingdom without being noticed. Ravenswood Kingdom was devoid of foliage of any kind. It appeared to be their strategy for keeping their people in subjection. There was no place to hide.

The Castle sat high on a hill with nothing but barren country surrounding it. You could see for miles in any direction. Any type of insurrection would be noticed immediately.

The valet took a few minutes to consider this proposal. "It will not be easy freeing her. The Prince only allowed her to visit the stables after he learned that she could not ride. I am sure that is the only reason he is letting me bring her mare to her."

It was hard for Prince Carlton to conceal his anger. "He has not hurt her has he?"

"No, not that I am aware of. He is trying to convince her to marry him. She was meant to marry Prince Carlton, but he would not have her. At least that is what the servants say."

"Prince Carlton would not have her?" Carlton did not mean to raise his voice, but he was astonished to hear this news, first from the stable boy and now from Henry's servant.

"Yes, Millie, a servant in the kitchens here at the inn told us that Princess Caroline only came to Ravenswood because Prince Carlton sent her flowers telling her he only wanted to be friends, that he could never love her."

Now Carlton understood what his mother was talking about. He chastened himself for not paying attention to his mother's advice. Caroline was like his mother, the flowers spoke to her. *What had I sent her? I told Clara to choose some pink, pretty flowers. Didn't she know I can't*

*communicate with flowers? What about my note? Surely
that did not say I only want to be friends?*

Pushing all that aside, Carlton said, "I believe we are on the
same side! May we accompany you to the castle?"

"What shall I tell my men?"

"Are they of the same mind, politically, as you are?"

With a laugh, the man said, "No! They would kill the
Prince if given the opportunity. I believe that the Prince is
not wholly bad, but I side with the people."

"Then I suggest that you send them on to Breckridge Hall,
and tell the Kings of our plan. I will scribe a note for them
to deliver to King Stefen. They will not suspect anything if
you left as three riders and return just the same. Once we
get to the castle, you can introduce us to those who are not
loyal to your King and we will prepare the arrival of King
Stefen. We will be ready to travel whenever you are."

"Perfect! They would savor such a venture and no one
need be the wiser. After they have delivered your note,
they will wait here at the inn until you or I return. We will
leave within the hour."

With a nod of approval Carlton turned to leave, then as an
afterthought he said, "King Stefen may ask them to be their
guide to enter into the Kingdom, would they be willing to
do that?"

"Of course, they would do anything if it meant they could
free themselves and their families from this King!"

After scribing a note and with his ring, sealing it with wax, all of the men left the Inn. It would be a long night, but Carlton could not wait a minute longer to go to Caroline's aide.

Part 13

Caroline sat in a window that overlooked the barren country. She couldn't remember seeing a flower or smelling any fragrances besides dirt or smoke since she arrived. *How could anyone enjoy this kingdom? How can I ever have gotten myself into such a mess as this? I have been here for only two weeks, yet it felt like an eternity. Never again will I take my family for granted. If I am ever to be free of this place, I will have to be cunning.*

Her lady in waiting was of little help. However, this scatter brained servant was to blame for this whole escapade. She did not know how to fulfill a simple request. Prince Carlton had given her the mission to deliver his note to Princess Caroline along with some flowers. The girl forgot about the note and delivered only the flowers. The note had been in her apron. Caroline found the note herself after they had arrived in Ravenswood.

When she asked Clara about it, she turned red. "I forgot about it, milady, and then I was afraid you would be mad, so I just kept it."

Dearest Caroline,

I have been sent on an errand by the King. I would have bid farewell to you in person, however, I could not trust myself to say the things that are in my heart. And so I must trust your lady in waiting to do my bidding for me.

I know that I have not been what you desired in a companion for life. I have been all of the things you told me the first day I met you in the kitchens at Breckridge Hall. A spoiled, selfish, fop. A poor excuse for a prince. And were it not for you that is what I would have remained.

Your words, harsh as they may have been, caused me to look not only inward, but I have also seen a side to my parents and our people that I had never bothered to see before. I pray that you have seen a change in me and my behavior.

What I am trying to say is that I love you. I love the way I feel when you are with me. I cannot imagine living without you. When I return, I hope that you will allow me to show you the man that I have become because of you.

Affectionately,

After Caroline had read the note, she wanted nothing more than to be back in her home in Breckridge Hall. The note contained exactly what she needed to give her the courage necessary to save herself and endure.

Only a few days earlier she had asked Prince Henry about her horse, Ginger. He reluctantly told her that he had placed her horse in the care of a master horseman. "Don't worry your pretty little head over her! We have plenty of horses here if she does not pull through."

Caroline did not like being treated like a child, or a helpless woman. However, she did know how to use the situation to her advantage. "You see, Your Highness, the mare was a gift to me from the Queen of Cantwell. It was her horse. She knows that I cannot ride, but enjoy the beauty of the animals. Once on a visit to Cantwell, she allowed me to curry her horse, and I found great comfort in that. I am used to spending most of my days in the gardens and in the mews. It would give me great comfort to be able to care for my horse."

"You cannot ride? Why not?"

"I never learned, Your Highness. I suppose my mother thought it was un-ladylike." Playing stupid was Caroline's best ally.

"I will send for your horse right away, if it will bring you happiness. I had no idea that you were so attached."

Prince Henry is educated, but not with regards to women. He is dull, boring and full of false pride.

Caroline suspected that her lack of ability to ride a horse had a great deal to do with his willingness to have her horse brought to the castle stables.

She had spent many hours walking the barren grounds of Ravenswood searching for an escape. Caroline knew that her only hope was Ginger. Oh, how she prayed that Ginger would be returned to her in good health.

As Caroline reflected on her *visit* to Ravenswood, she grew angry at the King. He had summoned her to his bedside and excused all of his servants. Laying there on his bed, he told her that she would never leave Ravenswood. He did not give her any details or excuses. No explanation or hope.

"So I have been brought here under false pretenses? Carried off and taken captive?"

As King Norman lay in his bed, seeing her shock, he laughed. "I knew I would best them in time. I didn't think it would take this long, I have been planning this for over 30 years! Your parents, and King Stefen, stole my Kingdom from me."

Before Caroline could say anything, he continued. "It was only hours away, King Stefen and Queen Lydia would wed and I would gain the throne of Cantwell without lifting an arm!"

Forgetting Caroline was present, or so it seemed, he continued to rant. "That stupid Minstrel! I silenced him for sure. And, now I have used him for my own purposes."

At that, Caroline could not help but look confused. "The minstrel works for you?" Caroline was surprised. She knew that the minstrels sang for money but did not know that they could be made or paid to sing a particular song.

This seemed to please the King and so he continued, "Yes! I know that the minstrel told King Markus of my plan to claim Cantwell. I found that fool of a minstrel and I now keep his family here in the castle dungeons. He now sings a different tune! Whatever tune I please!"

"Henry did not want to use the minstrel, but seeing how well they are received, especially at Breckridge Hall, I felt it necessary and an integral part to my plan."

Then he turned toward her and stared. "How do you think Henry came to learn of your beauty, your determination not to marry the fop, Prince Carlton and your parents release from the betrothal?"

"The minstrel? He seemed so kind and true."

"Well lass, let that be a lesson to you! Not everyone is what they seem."

The King rang a bell and several servants came in cowering. "Yes, Your Majesty?"

"Send for the minstrel!"

"Yes, Sire."

Moments later the minstrel entered. He looked apologetically at Caroline and then bowed his head, "Yes your majesty?"

"Sing your song of Ravenswood."

The Minstrel then sang a song of love and beauty.

Laughing the King demanded, "Sing of Princess Caroline."

The Minstrel picked up his mandolin, faced Caroline and began to play.

"Princess Caroline of Breckridge Hall,

Definitely the Bell of the Ball!

A genuine lady of Royal Birth,

To win her heart, 'twould be of great worth.

Prince Carlton wants to win her heart,

Poor lad is off to a miserable start.

She has a mare, 'twould rival any,

To learn to ride, she would give plenty.

Common knowledge is her love of flowers,

In her gardens she spends hours.

Take care, Prince Henry must act fast,

Her disdain for Prince Carlton won't long last."

Then, with a bow the minstrel handed Princess Caroline a begonia.

His song spoke of a spunky princess who does not cower, but will turn her head for lace and flower. The minstrel puzzled her. His songs may be the reason she was here, but he appeared to be acting on her behalf. Caroline had heard his song of Ravenswood. That was part of the reason she had agreed to come with Prince Henry for the King's supposed birthday celebration. "Is that all of it?"

The minstrel nodded his head and said, "Yes, Your Highness. That is all."

Caroline was relieved to know that the minstrel had not sung of her ability to ride a horse or her hobby of communicating with flowers. For these were her only hopes of escape.

The King's laugh brought Caroline back to the present. He rang for the servants and dismissed Caroline.

As Caroline left the kings chamber, she couldn't help but wonder where the minstrel had found a flower, here in Ravenswood. She slowly walked back toward her apartments. Out of the corner of her eye she saw a sprig of thyme laying on the floor just below a beautiful tatted wall hanging. As she picked up the twig, she noticed the unique design in the paneling beneath the fabric covering. She had only seen this symbol at Cantwell, yes! Cantwell Kingdom had a similar design. Remembering the days spent with Carlton in Cantwell and the sprig of Thyme gave her added courage. This king and kingdom, has not won yet!

Seeing she was alone, she carefully lifted the fabric. In the light from above she could make out a two-headed eagle. Looking just above the eagle, she saw a round carving about the size of a biscuit. Again, she looked around her to make sure that she was alone. Hoping that this wall mimicked the one in Cantwell, she pressed on the round carving with all of her strength. Hearing a click, she stepped in as a door opened. She quickly closed the door behind her. Just inside was a lit candle and another sprig of thyme. Someone was trying to lure her out of the castle. Whoever it was, knew she could communicate with flowers. The only person she could think of was the minstrel.

Hadn't he been to the Tournament? Surely he could have gathered flowers in Breckridge or Cantwell for that matter. It only took her a minute to decide whether or not she would follow the trail being laid before her. *What do I have to lose?*

With the candle in her hand, she followed the winding hallway. It led to stone steps. The passage was large enough for only one person and each step seemed to echo. As she continued to descend the stairs, she felt the dampness of the dungeons and could hear the echoes of the past. This passage was probably built as an escape, should the castle be taken over by intruders. Caroline had to reign

146

in her imagination as she could hear the clanking of armor rushing down these stairs searching for escape, or the clattering of swords as the knight was met with a foe.

She had been to the dungeons before, she had found them the first week she had come to Ravenswood. Caroline brought what food she could take from the king's tables and had made it a daily routine. However, she had not seen this part of the dungeons. Finally she heard voices, men's voices, whispering and anxious.

"Here she is, Sire."

What? Was this a trap? Had the minstrel truly led her to the King?

Just as Caroline was about to turn around the minstrel called to her, "Princess Caroline, you are safe."

Against her better judgment, Caroline turned around. There stood the minstrel with a single yellow rose in one hand extended to her.

She winkled her forehead and made an observation, "Your song did not tell of my love of flowers and their meanings?"

"No, Your Highness, I am not a *loyal* subject of the king's, as you know, he holds my family hostage. My apologies for any part I may have played in your coming to Ravenswood."

Taking the offered flower, Caroline surveyed the dungeon. That is when she remembered that they were not alone.

There on a stool sat a man in rags that appeared to have been royal robes at one time.

The man, faint for want of food, bowed his head and whispered, "Milady."

Caroline bowed her head in response and inquired, "Who are you?"

"Prince or rather, King Broderick."

"Prince Henry's father? I heard you were exiled, but I never imagined you were imprisoned. Your father is more evil than I had imagined!"

"Begging your pardon, Your Highness," the minstrel interjected, "the man you just spoke with is not the king. King Norman died twenty years ago."

"Then who?" Caroline asked perplexed.

"The Cardinal. He was in league with King Norman, but he is more evil than King Norman ever was."

"How long have you been held captive? What about the people? Surely they know that the Cardinal is not the rightful king."

King Broderick stood, and offered his stool to Caroline. It was not until he stood that she saw the iron and chains that held him captive. She hesitated and then not wanting to deny him this act of chivalry, she sat down. It had obviously been some time since he had company and she was not going to let him see the pity she felt for him.

"My father, like the cardinal, never allowed his subjects to enter the castle. Or to have an audience with him. None of them would recognize him, especially now that the cardinal has aged. Why even my own son, thinks he is being mentored by his loving grandfather."

"Surely Prince Henry does not condone his actions. Does Henry know you are down here?"

"No, of that he is innocent. When he was sent away to school, my father told me Norman was ill and of the scheme he and the cardinal had planned. He also made me aware of my fate. He gave me my choice of exile for my wife. I sent her away. I could not bear the thought of Marianne being imprisoned, too."

"Surely she didn't agree, no woman would leave her husband just to satisfy here own selfish desires."

"Before you think too harshly of her, I never told her of my exile. I told her I needed my space and that our marriage was a mistake. I told her to go with Henry. He attended school near where her family is from. It allowed her to be with him on holidays."

Caroline was amazed as she listened to King Broderick relate his sorted tale. "You are nothing like your father," the Princess curtsied to the king and stood to leave. Looking at the minstrel she said, "Surely you have not led me down here without a plan. What would you like me to do?"

"Rumor has it that your betrothed is helping the people over-throw the cardinal. The people are not aware of King

Broderick's circumstances or whereabouts. When it happens we need someone who can speak freely to the new king. Someone who will convince them to free King Broderick."

"Why haven't you told King Stefen or my father about King Broderick's imprisonment? You have been to both kingdoms!"

"My family is being held hostage. If I were to participate, they would be the first to suffer. I know it sounds cowardice, but I could not live with myself if they were hurt any worse than they already are. The people are not aware of my family's circumstances. I am afraid, they believe me to be a traitor," said the minstrel with bowed head.

Caroline felt sympathetic, "when I have visited the other dungeons, I noticed they have access out of the castle without ever going into the main parts of the castle. This passage was obviously built as an escape route. Do either of you know where it leads?"

King Broderick pointed to a solid cement wall with a fireplace in the center of it.

"Through the stack?"

"No, milady, turn the iron handle just right of the fireplace.

With great effort, Caroline turned the handle. As she turned the wall began to shift opening up another passage way. When it was large enough to enter, the King stopped her. "No need to examine it further, it leads to the mews.

It will come up through the floor to the Royal mews. It was planned that way to aide in the escape, should there ever be need of one."

"How does one open this door from the other side?"

"There is a handle just like this on the other side. Once they come in from the mews, we can leave either route."

"Your Majesty, I have been in the mews and I have not seen the door that you have described."

"Look on the floor in the back portion of the mews. It is most likely covered with a thick carpet of straw. I doubt that the Horse Master is even aware of its existence."

"I will bring you food later, if I can. I had better get back or they will suspect something."

King Broderick smiled and settled back down on his stool. Caroline walked back up the passage way. She was very careful to listen before she opened the secret door.

The feelings inside the castle were nothing like the feelings she had felt in the barren countryside. The sentiment in the country was one of sorrow and despair. The mood in the castle was one of hate and wickedness. It was hard for Caroline to understand or describe. It was foreign to her.

Now as she sat at the window, she could see the road toward Cantwell, barren and black. She spent a good portion of her days here, waiting for the return of the three servants who had gone to collect Ginger. Finally, today, she saw three riders coming. Three riders and four horses, Ginger was with them.

Tears welled up in her eyes, thoughts and emotions flooded her mind. Carlton headed her parade of memories. She began with the conversation before she even knew who he was. *That was embarrassing, yet dear to my heart. It had made such a difference for them both.*

Then there was horseback riding. What beautiful days – whether he knew it or not, Carlton had ridden deeply into my heart as he taught and prepared me, although unknowingly, for the most important ride of my life. The ride away, the escape from Ravenswood.

She wanted to be almost anywhere but Ravenswood, and so she encouraged her thoughts to return to anything and everything that involved Carlton. He was what she longed for, he made her feel safe and he treated her as an equal. She loved him. Now, how was she going to get to him and tell him to his face?

Seeing Ginger, was the first bit of comfort Caroline had received in weeks. First Carlton's letter and now Ginger. If only her note had made it to Breckridge Hall. But she mustn't dwell on that - one step at a time. Ginger would soon be here and she would provide that small bit of hope that Caroline needed to see her through. She watched through her window, until she could no longer see the riders. Then she grabbed a shawl and headed for the mews.

Carlton knew that Caroline would be in the stables if at all possible when the mare arrived. For this reason, he and his valet did not go to the royal mews, but to the servant's stables instead. While he wanted to see Caroline, he dared not jeopardize their escape. Knowing that his father would not arrive for a few more days, Carlton would need to keep himself apart from his beautiful princess. When the time came, he would let her know he was near. Until then, he must keep his distance.

Carlton was grateful for the near, but dilapidated barns. They allowed him to seclude himself and still watch Princess Caroline as she hurried to see Ginger. *I had almost forgotten how beautiful she is. It is refreshing to see her and her excitement to see Ginger. I have to free her.*

"Where are the men who came with you, John?" Princess Caroline asked as she stroked her horse.

"They had other matters to attend to, Your Highness."

"Of course! Please convey my deepest appreciation to them both, she looks beautiful!" Caroline took the reins and led the horse into a stable that had been prepared for her. As she brushed and curried the horse she hummed.

Prince Carlton found himself daydreaming as he listened to Princess Caroline care for the mare. The horse leaned into the Princess enjoying the attention. No doubt that Ginger had missed the Princess, almost as much as Caroline had missed her.

Forcing himself to leave, Carlton and his valet had much to do to prepare for the arrival of his father and King Markus.

Part 14

There was no doubt in the Monarchs' mind of what should be done. The knights had returned with their report only to be followed an hour later with Prince Henry's two men, the notes from Princess Caroline and Prince Carlton.

Queen Lydia told them the meaning of the flowers and seeds that Caroline had requested. All of which expressed her concern and desire to return home.

The men from Ravenswood confirmed King Stefen's other reports, King Norman and Prince Henry were facing an insurrection, and rightly so. Their actions were not in accord with a worthy Monarch. A King must care for his subjects, not exploit them. King Markus knew that they would need to support the people if they wanted to save lives. Not only that, but they must return Caroline unharmed.

Prince Everett was still in no condition to travel. His leg was healing, but would require more time before he could ride a horse. He was able to walk with the assistance of a staff, but he would only slow them down. He knew it. He hated it. Everett's every move pained him. He could not help but think, *Prince Henry was not a gentleman, rather a scoundrel, cunning and calculating.*

King Stefen rode ahead to ready his knights. King Markus would join him as soon as provisions could be secured. Queen Hannah decided to stay at Breckridge Hall with Queen Lydia. Here they would anxiously await the news.

"She will be fine, Lydia, I am sure of it!" Hannah comforted her best friend.

"Caroline is a bit stubborn. I just hope she does not anger the King to a point where he causes her harm."

"I am sure she will be fine. She is very smart as well – she knows there is trouble and a danger – she will act appropriately. King Norman does not want a war, I am sure. He knows that she is your beloved daughter, surely he will not harm her."

"I hope not. If Markus feels that she has been injured in any way, he will not deal kindly with the King. She is his pride and joy."

"I have seen him with her, I believe every father should have a daughter such as Caroline." Even as she spoke the words, Hannah's heart ached. She had lost their only daughter just weeks before she was to be born. Oh, how her heart and arms still ached for that child.

Seeing that Hannah was hurting, Lydia changed the subject. "Let's go ready the garden for their return. It may not matter to the men, but Caroline will want to visit the gardens when she gets home. Especially if Ravenswood is as desolate as their reports."

It was good for the women to have something to do. The flowers always brought them joy. Soon they were reminiscing on their younger carefree days as girls. They spent many hours in the garden. Pruning and cultivating, both busily working and enjoying the solace of true friendship. Although their families were in danger, they would comfort and cheer one another until the conflict was over.

Carlton spent the next few days, talking with servants and canvasing the inside of the castle. He examined it thoroughly, except for the parts that were occupied by the royal family. He made particular note of the dungeons and the secret escape routes pointed out by the castle staff. Their willingness and obvious hope encouraged the Prince.

He was shocked by the number of people living in the dungeons. Most of which were there as a ploy to keep their families under subjection. This he decided should be the first place to come after his father arrived. Not that these people would be of any help, they were mostly starved, barely kept alive on scones, water and gruel on occasion. However, once they were out of the dungeons, the people outside the castle would be free to act, knowing that their family members were no longer in danger. Carlton had spoken with them and had given them directions on how to leave the castle once the cell doors were opened.

The Captain of the Guard was a strong ally of the King. Carlton had been informed of those whom he could trust and those whom he could not. The insurrection was now in place, just waiting for the support from Cantwell and Breckridge Hall Kingdoms. Once they arrived, it would be a quick takeover- at least Carlton hoped it would. What would happen to Ravenswood after the takeover, he did not know. Again, he was grateful for his father. This was a decision Carlton did not want to make.

A week after Carlton had arrived in the Ravenswood Castle, he received word that his father was ready to meet and discuss strategies with him. One of the couriers was the man he had met at the Inn. They had led King Stefen and his men in through a secret pass-the only one that could not be seen from the castle.

They led Carlton to a cottage a short distance from the castle. There in the cover of the night Carlton joined in the issuing of weapons of every kind to the peasants. Worried that they might run out of weapons, King Stefen asked if they had any of their own.

A man, in his sixty's, obviously suffering from a life of servitude, answered, "We are not permitted to have weapons of any kind. The King's guards collected anything that could be used as a weapon and took them to the Castle. They are in the dungeons."

King Stefen looked at Carlton as if to ask if that was correct. "I haven't seen them in the part of the dungeons I have been in. Sir, do you happen to know exactly where they are stored?"

"Yes, just below the King's quarters, he stores all of his treasures there. Or perhaps I should say all of the treasures of the Kingdom."

"I will look into it," Carlton said to his father. "They will come in handy when it begins. What are your plans?"

Stefen pulled Carlton aside and asked for his opinion. "Do you think these people are willing to follow another Monarch? Or will this lead to disaster?"

Sensing the Kings concern, the same servant came forward. "Sire, we only need a leader! We desire freedom from oppression. We are not a blood thirsty people."

So, King Stefen asked the spokesman plainly, "Are you willing to follow another King? What do you hope to do with your Kingdom once you have conquered the King and his grandson? Who will reign as King? What are your intentions?"

Just then, the Prince Henry's valet came forward. "Your Majesty, I believe I speak for the people when I say that we are not opposed to royalty. Only those who abuse their position. We are well aware of your kingdoms and the people in them. They love their kings and are happy living as subjects. We believe that Prince Henry, if given the proper guidance, could be a good King. He has only returned from a life outside this last six months. He is still learning his place. With good leadership, he may be able to one day be our King.

This surprised both King Stefen and Prince Carlton. Stepping toward the people, King Stefen asked, "Does this man speak the mind and will of all of you here? Speak now or hold your peace."

All of the men grunted their approval.

"So be it!" said the King. "We will take control of the Castle and anyone who opposes us. Then we will negotiate the future of the Kingdom with Prince Henry. If he is willing to listen to the voice of his people, we will allow him to rule, subject to King Markus' and my approval if that is your wish, until such time as the people of the kingdom have confidence in him. Additional details of this agreement will evolve with time." For the first time in many years, the people had a common goal and hope in their future.

For the first time in many years, the people had a common goal and hope in their future. This time, the people cheered in agreement.

Pulling Carlton aside, the King whispered to Carlton, "Princess Caroline must be out of the castle and free before the takeover. Have you found a way to get her out without alerting the Prince?"

"Yes, Father. Every morning she comes to the stables to care for Ginger. She is there before breakfast. I can arrange for my valet to saddle her horse and take her to safety."

"No, not your valet son, you."

"I cannot leave you here to do this alone."

"I am not alone, son. Markus will be here and I have my men. I am not sure who we can really trust. If anything were to happen to the Princess, neither you nor I would ever forgive ourselves. Saddle your horse, too, and take her to Breckridge Hall. Her mother and yours are anxious for her return."

"Father, who will help you get into the castle? I have learned all of the passage ways."

"Have you recorded them?"

"Yes."

"Hand them to me. These men are fighting for their freedom. They will aide me, at least until they know that we have gained control. Markus is coming with his knights. They are double what I have brought with me. We will be fine."

"I confess, there is nothing I would like more that to take my beautiful princess home!"

"Then do it, son! I will have provisions for you and the princess waiting here. Take Thomas with you. He is a good man, and one I trust. I knew his father and his father before him. Don't stop until you have reached Cantwell. Only stay there long enough to rest your horses. Then move quickly to Breckridge Hall. Your valet and a guard will follow close behind you as an added protection. Do you understand?"

"Yes, father, what about her servant, Clara?"

"Does she normally go to the stables with Caroline?"

"No, she does not."

"Then we will take care of her. She will be fine. She will be of no interest to the Prince or the King. The way they treat their subjects, they can only expect that we do the same. She is in no real danger."

"Good luck, father! Do you have a message for Mother?"

"Just tell her I love her and I will be home soon."

They clasped forearms, their glance was one of mutual respect and trust.

Turning to the armed peasants, the king said, "Sleep well tonight men, for tomorrow, we will infiltrate the castle from the underground tunnels. We will free the prisoners, arm them and take control of the castle before King Markus and his men are in view from the castle entrance."

Impressed by the confidence these men placed in his father, Carlton went back to the stable. He doubted any of them would enjoy sleep tonight. He would spend the night there waiting for Caroline to come feed Ginger in the morning.

Caroline woke early the next morning. It had been a sleepless night, with dreams of rides with Carlton at Cantwell. She remembered the view of Breckridge Hall and before she broke into sobs she prepared to go to the stables. She wanted nothing more than to spend time with Ginger. Ginger reminded her of all of the beautiful things that she had taken for granted at Breckridge Hall.

Of a truth, she had been judging Prince Carlton too harshly. She realized that some of the faults she had accused him of were ones that she too shared.

She had been a spoiled, selfish child. Perhaps her parents coddled her more than they should have. She had never wanted for anything. The only thing she was ever denied was horseback riding. Even in that, they were only trying to protect Caroline from what they believed could hurt her. She knew that if she were ever freed from this awful place, she would be a better person.

As she passed the King's study, she heard voices. At first she was tempted to listen, but thought better of it. She continued walking down the hall.

Suddenly, Prince Henry called to her. "Princess Caroline, where are you off to so early?"

"I couldn't sleep, Your Highness, I thought I would see to Ginger."

"Would you like some company?"

Caroline wanted nothing more than to be left alone, but didn't quite know how to say it without upsetting the Prince. Just as she was about to accept his company, a servant called to him.

"Your Highness, there is a matter that the King has asked you to resolve before breakfast."

He heaved a sigh, gave a nod of acknowledgement and turned to give a look of disappointment to Caroline.

She forced a disappointed smile and she continued on her way.

Apparently she was not the only early riser this morning. *Everyone seemed on edge, Caroline thought to herself. But then, they were always on edge here in this awful, Kingdom.*

As she reached Ginger's stall she found that her mare was missing. Seeing a servant, she called to him. "You there, where is my horse?"

Still shadowed by the dim lights of dawn, the servant pointed to the pasture.

Looking in the direction he pointed, Caroline saw Ginger in the paddock, saddled and ready to ride. Someone was leading her. "Wait, she yelled, what are you doing with my horse?"

Carlton turned around, seeing him, silenced her. "My darling, mount quickly! We are leaving right now."

A flood of emotions filled Caroline. She wanted to run into his arms and never leave. Somewhere in the back of her mind, she knew that this was not wise, she must do as he said. *There would be time for proper reunions after we are safe.*

Caroline had never ridden a horse wearing a full skirt, but now was no time to bother about proper riding attire. She gathered her skirts and with Carlton's aide she was secured on the saddle. It had been months since she had ridden, but she was ready and anxious to ride; she had missed it. But that was not all, she was finally going to escape, to freedom, home and true love.

"Stay close to me Caroline! Don't look back no matter what. Let's ride."

By the time Carlton and Caroline arrived at the cottage, the place where they were to meet Thomas, King Stefen and his men were already in the castle.

Carlton envisioned his father rushing through the tunnels, setting the prisoners free.   Carlton picked up their provisions and followed Thomas through the secret passage way. After they had been riding for an hour, they heard King Markus' knights heading toward the castle. Hearing them from such a distance comforted Carlton, as he knew that noise accompanied only sizable armies.

"Carlton, they will see them! You can see for miles from the castle!"

"Don't worry Caroline, my father and his men were in the castle dungeons before we even left the cottage. They have most likely already secured the Castle. Your father and his men are a show of force. We anticipate nothing more.

"We must go back!" All of the sudden, Caroline stopped her horse and headed toward the castle. Caroline was yelling so Carlton might hear.

"No, Caroline, you must go home! They will all be safe, all those who oppose the King are on our side. There are only a few inside the castle that will give them any resistance. Once they see that they cannot win, they will surrender."

"He is not the King!"

"What are you talking about?"

"The real King is King Broderick. He is in the dungeons, I have met him."

"Caroline! What were you doing in the dungeons?"

"I wandered down there one day and began taking food to the prisoners."

"I, too, have been in the dungeons, I never saw the King."

"He is separate from the other people. I don't believe that they know he is there. He is not in a regular cell. He is under the Cardinals room."

"The Cardinal? What has he to do with this?"

"The Cardinal and King Norman were in league with each other. They were about the same age. They ravaged their Kingdom. They are the ones who hoped to take over Cantwell, when your father and my mother were engaged.

"King Norman's son, then Prince Broderick, had become friends with your father. He challenged his father's intention of invoking their right to Cantwell's throne. I believe it was Prince Broderick that sent the Minstrel to tell my Father of King Norman's plans.

"After King Stefen and Hannah were married, King Norman became very bitter and banished his son. During this time the Prince met a beautiful woman, a commoner, they married. A year later she gave birth to their son, Prince Henry. Prince Broderick brought the child home to meet his grandfather. He was sure that King Norman would not disown him."

"The King took to Henry and all seemed well. When Henry turned eight he was sent to a boarding school. The King took ill and died shortly after Henry left. His death was known only to the Cardinal and his guard. He was buried in the dungeons near where King Broderick is kept.

"Then the Cardinal and King Norman's personal guard, locked King Broderick in the dungeon below the King's quarters.

"There he has remained for twenty years, and the Cardinal assumed the identity of King Norman. When the Cardinal became ill, he sent for Henry and pretended to be his grandfather. It had been so long since Prince Henry had seen his grandfather, he accepted the aging Cardinal as King and mentor. You see, we must tell them where the real King is."

"Caroline, I will see you safely home and I then will return to Ravenswood."

"No, Carlton! He will be concerned about his Kingdom! He will hear all of the noise and it's very possible that he will not be fed. Very few people know where he is. I will be fine. Leave me with Thomas. He will see me safely home. Please Carlton."

"Thorndyke, my valet, is following just behind. I will have him and his men take you home. Thomas is familiar with the castle and its passages. He will escort me to the Ravenswood."

After describing in detail, how to find King Broderick's cell, Caroline smiled and batted her eyes at Prince Carlton. "I shall see you in a few days. Thank you for coming for me!"

Carlton and Thomas rode as quickly as possible toward Ravenswood Castle. They took the shortcut one more time. The Prince was almost certain that the castle would be contained before he arrived, but he didn't want to take any chances. Once inside the castle he would free King Broderick.

They found King Broderick exactly where Caroline had described. He appeared a little weak, but was well enough to manage the back stairs to the Throne room. Once inside they easily found the main body of King Stefen's men.

They passed the Captain of the Guard, he was in chains along with several others who resisted. Thomas, King Broderick and Prince Carlton moved through the soldiers toward the King's private chambers.

King Stefen and his personal guard had already moved into the king's chambers. Unchained, but followed closely behind, Prince Henry was surrounded by guards from Cantwell. This was as much for his protection as anything. His subjects were now armed and there was no telling what they would do in retaliation.

Meanwhile, Prince Henry was still trying to grasp all of the events of the day.

Assessing the situation, and knowing it would be vital that Prince Henry learn the truth from the Cardinal himself,

King Broderick and Prince Carlton went in to join those in the Cardinal's chambers.

The Cardinal laid in his bed and laughed, "So, who have we here? Henry what is going on?"

Prince Henry sheepishly replied, "Grandfather, King Stefen has taken over the castle and our kingdom."

The Cardinal, only laughed as a small armed guard surrounded his bed. "King Stefen of Cantwell! I had hoped to meet you one day." His confidence was replaced by wrenching and coughing.

Before King Stefen could respond, Carlton, Thomas and the liberated King Broderick, entered the room. "Stefen!"

"Broderick! What has happened?"

Just then Prince Broderick saw his son. "Henry?"

Prince Henry looked confused until he looked closer into his father's eyes. "Father?"

King Stefen allowed Broderick and Henry a moment before asking, "Broderick, where have you been?"

Clasping Stefen's forearm, King Broderick said, "This is the Cardinal, he and King Norman were confederates."

King Stefen, relieved to see Broderick, said, "I have inquired of your whereabouts, however, no one knew. I was told you were exiled."

"After my father died twenty years ago, the Cardinal and his men sent me to an exile of sorts. I have been in the dungeons just below this room.

"Thank you, Stefen and Markus! Thank you for rescuing me and my kingdom." Then turning to the townspeople, King Broderick said, "I am truly sorry for your suffering of the past. If you will allow me, I would like to be your King."

The people all cheered. Learning of the close ties between King Stefen and King Broderick strengthened the hope and confidence in a bright future. The people took a great leap of faith in restoring King Broderick to power. They had confidence in King Stefen and King Markus. They knew that the two, would be more vigilant regarding their neighboring kingdom. Rebuilding would not be easy and if it was not done correctly, they knew they had allies.

Now that the real King had been restored to his throne, Carlton was free to attend to his other duties. That of Caroline!

He immediately excused himself and headed toward Breckridge Hall. This time he would not bring flowers or a note. But he would go on bended knee and beg the lovely Princess Caroline to be his bride.

Part 15

As Caroline approached Breckridge Hall, the trumpets blew announcing her arrival. She knew with all that had happened both her mother and Queen Hannah would be watching her as she rode into the main courtyard. She had no desire to hurt them, but she loved riding too much to give it up because of an accident that had happened so many years ago.

Just as she had expected, the Queens were waiting for her at the entry of the Castle. Princess Caroline began to apologize for concealing the fact that she knew how to ride a horse, and took the opportunity to thank Hannah for the gift of Ginger.

"Nonsense! My dear! We are grateful that you were able to escape. Are you all right?" Queen Hannah was very sincere.

"Who taught you to ride? Surely you have not become so familiar with a horse in just the few days it took you to get here." Queen Lydia was more curious than concerned.

"Prince Carlton, but you mustn't be angry with him. I beseeched him to teach me when I stayed at Cantwell. It wasn't until he gave me this horse that we learned why you had forbidden me to ride. I am so sorry for your loss Queen Hannah, but I don't want to give up riding. It is one of the things that Carlton and I have enjoyed doing together."

Queen Hannah put her arm around Caroline, "As far as I am concerned dear, you may ride whenever you desire.

Seeing you ride in just now, reminded me of the many times that Lydia and I had enjoyed a beautiful ride in the country. I could never ask you to give that up. Just promise to be careful."

"Thank you, I shall." Caroline looked at her mother, waiting for her consent.

Queen Lydia smiled and drew her daughter in, "You were never much of a one to obey my counsel! When Carlton brought you the mare, I suspected you had learned to ride."

Seeing the look of surprise on Caroline's face, Lydia continued, "A mother sees and hears more than you expect. The servants are very informative, too. Today, we are all very grateful that you can ride! It allowed you to come home safely."

"Have you any news of the conflict?" It wasn't until he spoke that Caroline realized Prince Everett was there with them.

Caroline quickly explained all that Carlton had shared. She told of the Cardinal's treachery and of King Broderick's imprisonment. They were relieved to hear that they expected very little confrontation, as the people of Ravenswood were aiding them in regaining their Kingdom.

"It will take some time for the Kingdom to recover from all of the damage that the Cardinal has done. There is so much suffering."

"Perhaps we can aide them. You asked for seeds perhaps that is just what they need. Seeds of not just flowers, grains and vegetables, but seeds of support and confidence in a bright future!"

It was then that Caroline realized that communicating with flowers was not just a fun secret for the Queens, but it meant more to them. They used the beauty of the flowers to comfort, encourage and strengthen not only each other, but everyone in their Kingdoms. They truly wished everyone to experience the joy that they had each found in serving and loving.

"Come in dear, it's been a hard journey and we have much to discuss." Queen Lydia led the way and they each followed in turn.

Everett, lingered on the porch, hoping that Caroline's tale was true. *Could such a conquest really be that simple?* Everett spent the next day sitting on the veranda of the East Tower. The view from here allowed him to see riders from the South when they were still quite a distance away. He was frustrated that he was not able to help his father when he was needed. Lydia knew he was healing because of his mounting irritations.

Finally, the following afternoon, he saw dust in the distance. Riders were coming, a good number of them. Snatching his looking glass, he searched the group of men for any sign of recognition. They were all soldiers, but it was not clear where they hailed from. Just as Everett was about to warn the castle guards, he saw a lone rider break through the line at a full speed.

Prince Everett chuckled. *Prince Carlton! I should have known he would be first to the castle. Poor man has fallen in love!* Knowing how long it would take him to descend the stairs, Everett waved to the watch tower and had them delay the warning blow. He felt Carlton and Caroline deserved a private reunion. If the trumpeter blew, all of the castle would be on alert and Caroline would leave the gardens.

Leaving his vigil, Everett went to greet Carlton and the other men. He wanted to be the one to open the door for the conquering heroes. Carlton was the first to arrive. Everett caught the discarded reigns of Carltons horse and slapping Carlton on the back Everett, said, "You'll find her in the gardens."

The proposal that Carlton had been formulating was weighing heavy on his mind. What to say, how to say it, he was drawing a blank. She relies on flowers more than words. How does one compose a proposal bouquet? All he wanted was to hold her in his arms. *Perhaps that is why his mother had turned to flowers. They can speak when words are not good enough.*

As he entered the garden, he realized that he was out of breath. Had he literally been running to see her? *What must she think?* However, when he saw her, he knew that words were not necessary. She ran to him and they embraced. Tears ran down her cheeks.

As he whispered in her ear, she could feel his breath on her neck. A chill rolled down her back. It took her a minute to realize he was speaking to her. "I need to create a bouquet. Will you help me?"

Pulling away just enough to see his face, she asked, "What do you want it to say?"

"Love, beauty, forever, vivacious, energetic, independent,

After cutting a few beautiful flowers she handed the bouquet to Carlton. Only letting go of one of her hands, he took the bouquet and slowly knelt on one knee. "My beautiful, Princess Caroline, will you please make me the happiest man on earth and be my bride?"

Smiling, she nodded and said, "Let me complete this bouquet. Since this is *our* wedding bouquet, I need to add a few more flowers. Let's see, courage, power, strength, and protection.

Suddenly, they heard the tower trumpeter blow, making the castle aware of the Kings' arrival. Hand in hand the Prince and Princess went to greet their fathers.

King Markus and King Stefen were not far behind Carlton. Their wives rushed to greet them and they all retired to the conservatory to share their tales with Prince Everett and their wives.

The main company of knights gathered in their quarters and would no doubt be recounting their tale to their fellow knights and the groomsmen. Before the day had ended every servant would know of the whole affair.

The end of this adventure ... the beginning of a new one!

Flowers and their Meanings

Acacia Blossom	Concealed Love, Beauty in Retirement, Chaste Love
Ambrosia	Your love is Reciprocated
Amaryllis	Pride, Pastoral Poetry
Anemone	Anticipation, Forsaken
Arbutus	Thee Only Do I love
Aster	Symbol of Love, Daintiness
Azalea	Take Care of Yourself for Me, Temperance, Fragile Passion
Bachelor Button	Single Blessedness
Begonia	Beware
Bells of Ireland	Good Luck!
Bittersweet	Truth
Bluebell	Humility
Camellia	Admiration, Perfection, Good Luck, Gift to Man
Camellia – Pink	Longing for You
Camellia – Red	You're a Flame in My Heart
Camellia – white	You're Adorable
Candy Tuft	Indifference
Carnation	Fascination, Divine Love
Carnation Pink	I'll Never Forget You
Carnation Purple	Capriciousness
Carnation Red	My Heart Aches for You, Admiration
Carnation Solid Color	Yes
Carnation Stripe	No, Refusal, Sorry I Can't be With You, Wish I Could be With You
Carnation white	Sweet & Lovely, Innocence, Pure Love
Carnation yellow	You have Disappointed Me,

	Rejection
Cattail	Peace, Prosperity
Chrysanthemum	You're a Wonderful Friend, Cheerfulness & Rest
Chrysanthemum Red	I Love You
Chrysanthemum White	Truth
Chrysanthemum Yellow	Slighted Love
Columbine or Aquilegia Canadensis	Means Foolishness (Because as a complete blossom, it resembles a Jester's Hat). Some people believe it is bad luck to give columbine to a woman. (However, as each individual petal with spur attached falls from the plant they look like a dove or a lady's slipper.) This is used in reference to the Holy Ghost or to the Virgin Mary.
Columbine Purple.	Resolve to Win
Columbine Red	Anxiousness
Coreopsis	Always Cheerful
Crocus	Cheerfulness
Cyclamen	Resignation & Good-bye
Daffodil	Regard, Friendship, Unrequited Love, You're the Only One, New Birth, New Beginning
Daisy	Hope, Love, Cheer
Dandelion	Faithfulness, Happiness
Dead Leaves	Sadness
Deadly Nightshade	Falsehood
Fern	Magic, Fascination,

	Confidence & Shelter
Fir	Time
Forget-Me-Not	Forget-Me-Not
Forsythia	Anticipation
Gardenia	You're Lovely, Secret Love
Garlic	Courage, Strength
Geraniums	Stupidity, Folly
Gladiolus	Symbolizing Strength and Moral Integrity, Infatuation, (In a bouquet conveys to recipient that they pierce the giver's heart with passion.)
Gladiolus	Strength of Character, Faithfulness & Honor, Remembrance
Gloxinia	Love at First Sight
Grass	Submission
Heather Lavender	Admiration, Solitude
Heather White	Protection, Wishes Will Come True
Holly & Holly Hock	Defense, Domestic Happiness
Hyacinth Purple	Sorrow, I am Sorry, Please Forgive Me
Hyacinth Blue	Constancy
Hyacinth Red or Pink	Play
Hyacinth White	Loveliness, I'll Pray for You
Hyacinth Yellow	Jealousy
Hydrangeas	Heartless
Iris (Fleur – de- lis)	Your friendship means so much to me, Faith, Hope, Wisdom & Valor, and My Compliments. Good News, Courage, Admiration
Iris (Fleur –de- lis)	Royalty

Dark Blue	
Iris Yellow	Passion
Ivy	Wedded Love, Fidelity, Friendship Affection
Ivy Sprig	Anxious to Please, Affection
Jonquil	Love Me, Affection Returned, Desire, Sympathy
Larkspur – Pink	Fickleness
Lavender Heather	Admiration
Lily	Majesty
Lily Calla	Beauty
Lily White	Chastity & Virtue
Lily Pink	Wealth & Prosperity
Lily Orange	Hatred
Lily Tiger Lily	Wealth, Pride
Lily, Stargazer	Wealth & Prosperity, Congratulations or I'm Sorry or Anything in-Between
Lily of the Valley	Happiness & Laughter
Magnolia	Nobility
Marigold	Cruelty, Grief, Passion & Creativity
Mistletoe	Kiss Me, Affection, To Surmount Difficulties
Monkshood	Beware, A deadly foe is near, Danger is Near
Moss	Maternal Love, Charity
Myrtle	Love
Narcissus	Egotism, Formality, Stay as Sweet as You Are
Nasturtium	Conquest, Victory in Battle
Nuts	Stupidity
Oleander	Caution
Orange Blossom	Innocence, Eternal Love

Orange Mock	Deceit
Orchid	Love, Beauty, Refinement, Beautiful Lady
Orchid Cattleya	Mature Charm
Palm Leaves	Victory & Success
Pansy	Loving thoughts, (Victorian meaning is "to think" particularly of love.)
Parsley	To remove bitterness
Peony	Shame, Happy Marriage
Petunia	Resentment, Anger, Your Presence Soothes Me
Pine	Hope, Pity
Poppy	Imagination
Poppy Red	Pleasure
Poppy White	Consolation
Poppy Yellow	Wealth; Success
Primrose	I Can't Live Without You
Primrose Evening	Inconstancy
Portae King	Daring
Rose – Coral	Desire
Rose – Dark Crimson	Mourning
Rose – Dark Pink	Thankfulness
Rose Lavender	Enchantment
Rose Leaf	You may hope
Rose Orange	Fascination
Rose - Pale Peach	Modesty
Rose Pale Pink	Grace, Joy
Rose – Red	Love, Respect
Rose- single in full bloom	I Love you, I Still Love you
Rose _ Tea	I'll Remember, Always
Rose – Thornless	Love at First Sight
Rose – White	Innocence & Secrecy
Rose – White and Red	Unity

Together	
Rose – Yellow	Joy, Friendship
Rosebud	Beauty & Youth, A Heart Innocent of Love
Rosebud Moss	Confession of love
Rosebud Red	Pure & Lovely
Rosemary	Love and fidelity. A token of remembrance
Sage	Symbol of strength and wisdom and immortality.
Smilax	Loveliness
Snap Dragons	Protect People from Deceit or Curses, Graciousness & Strength
Spider Flower	Elope With Me
Sweet Pea	Good-bye, Departure, Thank You for a Lovely Time
Thornless Rose Bud	Hope, I Fear no Longer
Thyme	Love and courage. Boost confidence
Tulip	Perfect Lover, Fame
Tulip Red	Believe me, Declaration of Love
Violet	Modesty
Violet – Blue	Watchfulness, Faithfulness, I'll Always Be True
Violet –White	Let's Take a Chance on Happiness
Viscera	Will You Dance With Me?
Zinnia – Magenta	Lasting Affection
Zinnia – Scarlet	Constance
Zinnia – White	Goodness
Zinnia – Yellow	Daily Remembrance
Zinnia – Mixed	Thinking or In Memory of

	an Absent Friend

Flower arrangements or Bouquets with meanings

Bouquet of withered Flowers = Rejected love

Columbine, day lily, broken straw, witch hazel and a daisy: Deceit and desertion. Deserted love. Breaking the spell of their attraction.

Lily of the valley & fern -Your unconscious sweetness has fascinated me.

Marigolds have been used in love charms. It was once thought to protect against the plague and to be effective in stopping gossip. The negative side can symbolize cruelty and jealousy. When used in combination with spells, the marigold is an anti-dote for the sharp tongued and promotes cheery conversations.

A small bouquet of pansies means think of me.

Parsley; to take away the bitterness, both physically and spiritually. Sage; strength for thousands of years. Rosemary; faithfulness, love and remembrance, sensibility and prudence. Thyme is for courage.

(Language of Flowers, website, thelanguageofflowers.com)

(Meanings & Legends of Flowers – C – angelfire.com/journal2/flowers/c1.html)

Glossary

Abdicate To relinquish (as sovereign power) formally. To renounce a throne.

Accomplice One associated with another, especially in wrong doing.

Alcove A small recessed section of a room; nook.

Arming Cap A small quilted cap worn under the mail coif that offered protection against blows and the friction of mail against the head.

Cabinet Private quarters for the royal men. Women's private quarters were called boudoirs.

Carriage A horse drawn vehicle designed for private use and comfort.

Castle A large fortified building or set of buildings. Charade An empty or deceptive act or pretense.

Curried To clean the coat of (as of a horse) with a curry comb.

Etiquette The conduct or procedure required by good breeding.

Façade A false, superficial or artificial appearance or affect.

Fop A man who is concerned with his clothes and appearance in an affected and excessive way; Dandy, Popinjay, Beau, Narcissus

Fording To cross (a body of water) by wading.

Fortnight A period of 14 days or 2 weeks.

Gait A sequence of foot movements by which a horse moves. (As a walk, trot, pace or canter.)

Gallantry   An act of marked courtesy.

Gaunt   Excessively thin and angular, often as a result of suffering.

Guarded   Cautious, circumspect.

Highwayman   A person who robs travelers on a road.

Hospitality   Given to generous and cordial reception of guests.

Imposter   One that assumes an identity or title not his own for the purpose of deception.

Incognito   With one's identity concealed or in disguise.

King   A male monarch of a major territorial unit.

Kingdom   A politically organized community or major territorial unit having a monarchial form of government headed by a king or queen.

Kings Guard Kings personal body guards.

Knight   A man honored by a sovereign for merit.

Lady In Waiting

Lady of a queen's or a princess's house hold appointed to wait on her.

Lord High Steward

Formerly, the first officer of the crown.

Mistress   A woman who has power or authority, or ownership.

Mount   To seat oneself (as on a horse) for riding. To go up; climb.

Nanny   A woman entrusted with the care and supervision of a child.

184

Paddock   An enclosed area used for pasturing or exercising animals.

Pomp   A show of magnificence; Splendor.

Prince   Son of a King or Queen.

Princess   Daughter or granddaughter of a sovereign.

Protocol   A code prescribing strict adherence to correct etiquette and precedence.

Queen   A female chieftain or a wife of a king.

Royal Mews Stables.

Settee   A long upholstered seat for more than one person, typically with a back and arms. Sofa, couch, divan, chaise longue, davenport.

Stone   Measurement of Weight - 14 pounds

Tea   In many parts of the British Isles, tea us used to mean the main   evening meal.

(Webster's Ninth New Collegiate Dictionary, Oxford Dictionary)

Acknowledgements

Writing is an adventure. We would like to thank Kiersten Nebeker, and Jenny Evans for your invaluable assistance in publishing the Prince Tales!

Elise Vowles, Elaine Crane, Beth Wooten, Nancy Stoker and Shelly Nowers, thank you!

Last of all, but certainly not least, we want to thank our husbands for their encouragement in all of our adventures.

Other books by the Authors:

At Last Ever After

The Empty Thorne

Rosie's Secret

The Quest

Never Invite a Giraffe to a Tea Cup Party

www.ingramcontent.com/pod-product-compliance
Lightning Source LLC
Chambersburg PA
CBHW072140170626
46813CB00004BA/1631